RACHEL CORD
Confidential Investigations

Still a Bitch

R. E. Conary

EQUAL
FOOTING
BOOKS

Everyone Deserves An Equal Footing

Second Edition

Still a Bitch

Rachel Cord
Confidential Investigations
Book 2

Copyright © 2015 R. E. Conary
Cover Photo © Diana Eller | Dreamstime.com—used by permission

Equal Footing Books
ISBN-13: 978-0692480328
ISBN-10: 0692480323

Previously published (2010) as
Rachel Cord, PI *'Still a Bitch'*

To all the women I've known and loved,
my heartfelt thanks.

One

ONCE THE CONVENIENCE store clerk stopped staring at my breasts, he recognized the man in the picture.

"Yeah, that's Mr. Carter. I see him with Mr. Stanley lots of weekends. They come in for gas and stuff. They usually order pizza on Saturday nights. A large double pepperoni, double cheese with hot peppers and onions. Not from here. I deliver for Pizza Quick at night. They're good tippers."

"Did you deliver a pizza last Saturday?"

He pulled his eyes back from staring at my breasts again. He was young, so I tried to ignore it. It happens all the time.

"No, they didn't call in an order. Didn't see them at all last weekend."

He gave me directions to Stanley's house and I thanked him. He strained over the counter to get a last look as I got into my car. I understood his interest. Every adolescent male from nine to 90 stares at my breasts. A lot of women do too, but that's a different story. I hate it, it's my albatross and there's little I can do about it—yet.

My breasts are huge. Double-H huge that stick out like the bullet bumpers on a fifties Buick. They're a cause of distraction, but more than that they're a pain: a pain in the neck and back just trying to stay upright, and a pain to the ego. It's automatically assumed that the bigger the breast the smaller the brain. But one of these days I'm getting them cut back to a pleasanter, more comfortable size: a C-cup at least, or, maybe a B. A girl has her dreams.

The mailbox was just as the clerk described, large and black with three blue reflectors on the post beneath it. I pulled into the dirt lane and stopped.

It rained heavily the past weekend washing the lane smooth. It didn't look like anyone had been here since. There were no tire tracks. This was Wednesday. Morning light through the trees turned the lane green as it twisted and curved through the woods. I couldn't see the house. I got out of the car and checked the mailbox. There were some letters and a magazine. One day's delivery? Three? What time of day? I had no idea. Only one of the letters had a readable cancellation from last week. No help there. I left them. It's against the law to tamper with other people's mail. I try not to break the law—too often.

The rain-swept lane told me Jerome Carter probably wasn't even here, or Kenneth Stanley either. Maybe they went fishing and hadn't yet returned. Maybe they had an accident. But they weren't in any hospital that I knew of, nor had any unclaimed bodies shown up. This could be a wasted trip. Still, I couldn't know for sure until I checked. Carter hadn't come home Sunday night and this is where his trail led.

Why was I here? Because I was hired to find the guy and hand him some papers? Because it's what I do for a living? Because I'm Rachel Cord, confidential investigator? Was that answer enough?

I didn't want to be here. Certainly wasn't welcome on this side of the river. I could have stayed in bed. Should have stayed in bed. Had plenty of reason to stay in bed and would be much happier there than here. I definitely didn't want to go down a tree-lined lane to a house hidden in the woods. Nasty things happen in such places. Nasty things that rip you apart, maybe never to be whole again. Nasty memories that didn't need to be dredged up.

Life isn't all hearts and flowers. It's pain and suffering too. It's an end and it's a beginning. It's dirty little secrets buried deep in the muck and mire below the surface where the grubs and worms feed. Secrets I unbury, like it or not. My business cards even say so: *"Life's a bitch. So am I."*

Yeah, that's why I was here: to prove to myself I can still handle it; that I'm still tough enough, hard enough. Bitch enough.

I started down the shimmering lane. Angled golden light pierced the green canopy sending up hazy mists that promised another hot, sticky, typical September start. The lane twisted around trees like a game trail instead of a driveway built by humans. The quiet crunch of tires on sand sent birds flittering and squirrels scurrying. The lane curved and as I crossed a short wooden bridge over a stream, I saw the log house at the crest of the hill across an open meadow. The meadow was wavy grasses and wildflower bursts of white and yellow, reds and blues. The colors extended up the hill toward the house, a modified A-frame with wings. A two-and-a-half story triangle of windows reflected blue sky.

The lane circled the meadow instead of cutting across straight to the house. There was a low place where the lane turned that still had a bit of water from the recent rains and looked pretty soft. No one had tried to drive through it or around it. I pulled to the left through the grasses to avoid getting stuck. Something scraped the undercarriage.

The lane curved up the rise and I saw the side of the house, two towering trees shading the back yard, and a log garage. The weathered gray logs shone in the sunlight. Beyond was more meadow with an old red barn and then the tree line. I stopped near the back of the house. A dark blue car parked in front of the garage was a late model Cutlass, and the license plate matched the information I had. I picked up the envelope of papers from the passenger seat and got out.

"Hello? Anyone home?"

A tawny tabby came out from beneath the deck to greet me. She meowed and rubbed herself against my leg. She leaned in hard as I rubbed her ears.

"You're a friendly kitty. Where is everyone?"

She looked at me with her deep amber eyes and meowed again.

I climbed the steps. An iron bell hung from a bracket beside the door. I rang it a couple of times. Its peal echoed across the meadow. The door was filled with glass panes. A cat door had replaced the bottom middle one. The room beyond was an enclosed porch with lots of windows. There were comfortable wicker chairs, a sofa and a table. An arrangement of wildflowers on the table needed to be replaced. I couldn't see into the rest of the house. The door was locked. Across the room, by the inner door, was a pair of metal bowls on the floor. They looked empty. The cat rubbed against my leg.

"Hey, did they go off and forget to feed you?"

She looked at me and opened her mouth silently. I knocked on the glass.

"Anyone here?"

No answer. All I heard were birds in the trees and the lazy buzz of a fat carpenter bee as it looked for a hole in the porch roof beam.

I stepped off the deck and away from the house. I couldn't see any open windows. The whir of a heat pump starting let me know that the electricity was still on and that it was probably a lot more comfortable in the house than out here. The air was already steamy from the hot sun sucking all the moisture out of the meadows. I wanted to get back into my air-conditioned car, get back to the city and my side of the river. This trip was a bust. I turned toward Carter's car and the garage. The car looked freshly washed from the rains. There were no tracks, so it hadn't been moved. The garage was built of the same weathered logs as the house. The two roll-up doors on the garage were closed. There was an open screened window on the side of the garage and a window set in the side door. I walked over to the door and put my face to the glass.

No cars in the garage. As I thought, Carter and Stanley must have left before the rains. Another window on the opposite wall also looked open. In the dim light I saw a workbench along one wall. Tools hung neatly from a pegboard. There was a sink and an old refrigerator. In the middle of the nearer car stall was a large dark mat on the floor. On it appeared to be a large beige lump that made me curious. I tried the door handle and it turned.

Despite the open windows, the room was stifling and reeked of fermenting shit and piss and stale sweat. My stomach flip-flopped and my breakfast threatened a return appearance. I fumbled for the light switch. My hand hit a button and then the switch. One of the garage doors began rising and the fluorescent lights flickered on. The dark mat turned an electric blue and the beige lump became a naked body curled in a fetal position with a brown leather ball for a head. Then I saw the chains.

(Chains bit into my arms and ankles stretching me, pulling my joints.) I couldn't breathe. (The electric blue silicone dildo smacked my bare belly.) I stumbled backward out the door, gagging. (I was being ripped, torn apart.) Leaned against the rough gray logs. (A bead of sweat clung precipitously to the tip of a taut nipple.) Slid down the wall, folding into myself. (An oblivious dark eye disappeared in the muzzle blast of an exploding cannon.)

Two

Two days earlier, I danced around the corner onto Cutter Avenue headed for Philadelphia Long's Tavern & English Tearoom. The weekend rains had cleaned the air and the sky was brilliantly blue. The humidity was up, but I didn't care. I was flying high. High, even though I was running late—which is something I hate. High for two reasons. First, and foremost, I was on my way to my first date in who knew how long. Second, I had just served papers to a guy who'd been making himself hard to catch. I scammed him using a tip from *PI Magazine*.

I had found where he'd been stashing his car, so I knew he was home. I walked up and knocked on the door of his condo. When he didn't answer, I knocked harder and called out loudly, "Robert Lewis, I know you're in there. You're not in trouble. This is about that accident you witnessed." I knocked again and nearly yelled, "Come on, Robert, open up."

The neighbors had to hear me and I didn't think the guy could tolerate that. Finally I heard movement and a voice called out from behind the door.

"Quiet down, will ya? There's no Lewis here."

Of course there was no Lewis. Robert Lewis was the

previous owner of this condo as I had found out at the County Tax Assessor's website.

"Look, Mr. Lewis, I know it was three years ago, but that accident you witnessed is finally going to trial, and the victim's lawyers really need your testimony. Open up, please."

He opened the door a crack. "I'm not Lewis, I tell ya. He moved. I bought this from him two years ago. Will you go away, now?"

I gave him my best I-don't-believe-you look. "Mr. Lewis, please, these people desperately need your help."

I held up the blank subpoena that I'd typed *Robert Lewis* on for him to see.

"No, seriously. Lewis moved, but I still get his mail sometimes."

"Okay, if you're not Lewis, who are you? If you can prove it, I'll leave."

He opened the door. "My name is Morehouse. Daniel Morehouse. Look here."

He pulled out a wallet and showed me his driver's license. I took it and compared the picture to his face.

"Gee, you're right, Mr. Morehouse. My apologies. This other subpoena must be for you." I handed him the real one with his license and turned to leave. "You've been served. Have a nice day."

He stepped into the hallway. "Hey, wait. What about Lewis?"

"Guess I'll have to keep looking for him."

So, here I was bouncing down Cutter Avenue on a hot sticky afternoon as happy as a lark and as nervous as a kitten amid a pack of Rottweilers. I danced into Phil's.

The Tearoom was crowded for a Monday: late summer tourists the week before Labor Day, four couples waiting to be seated. The women were talking together and pointing with their gloved hands at the large oil portraits of Queen Elizabeth II over the hearth and Princess Diana in the back draped in black. The men were standing around looking foolish and probably wishing they were at the tavern next door. Two of the men were stuck with god-awful courtesy ties that didn't match their short-sleeved shirts and shorts. At Philadelphia Long's English Tearoom ladies wear gloves and gentlemen wear ties.

I ducked into the ladies room. My hair was a mess. I was letting it grow out, and it was at that awkward stage where there was little I could do with it. I liked the new color, a rich auburn, but stylish it wasn't. I should have worn a wig. I have enough of them. I ran a quick brush through my mop—who was I kidding—and checked for any spots on my blouse or jacket and that there weren't any sweat stains showing. There was little point in wasting more time or worrying about that now; I was already late.

I slipped on a pair of ivory 2-button shortie gloves as Elspeth Glencannon returned from seating the party of eight.

"Rachel, it's great to see you. You've not been in in a while."

I liked the way her Highland burr rolled the R in my name. We hugged.

"Glad to see you too. I see the tourists are still flocking. I'm supposed to meet someone and I'm late. Do you know if she's here?"

"Aye, the dark-haired beauty near the back by the windows. She asked for you when she arrived." Elspeth looked at my hair. "Is this color new?"

"Yes. Do I look okay?"

"You look grand. Good luck to you."

"Thanks. I'll seat myself."

Most of the 12 lace-covered tables, as well as the three sitting areas by the windows and hearth, were occupied. Two tables were waiting to be cleared. Through the tall French windows I saw that many of the patio tables were also full even in this heat. It was good that the building shaded the patio and garden in the afternoon. Beneath the black-draped portrait of Princess Di a string trio played quietly.

Besides the odd tourist males, there were a couple of butches and bulls—wearing ties, of course, not gloves—with their ladies, but most of the crowd were femmes and lipsticks. Did the tourists realize the Tearoom was a lesbian hangout? Were we the attraction?

A couple of women gave me an inviting look and I smiled politely, but my concentration was on the "dark-haired beauty" as Elspeth called her.

She was looking out the window with her back to me. Her nearly black hair hung halfway down the back of her ice blue jacket. When was mine last that long? Light from the window added bright highlights and a few single threads of silver glimmered.

"Hi. Sorry I'm late."

I pulled out the chair by the window and began to sit. A face suddenly illuminated the shadows across the room. A haunting, beautiful, Japanese face. Karen? It was for just an instant; then the illusion burst. A busboy with a buzz cut stepped through the shadowed archway and went to the tables that needed clearing. He was slightly built and Karen's height, but there the similarity ended.

"Rachel? Rachel. Earth to Rachel; come in, please."

"What?"

"You were completely spaced out. Did you see a ghost?"

She turned to look at where I was staring. She turned back with a quizzical look. Her green eyes sparkled. I felt myself blushing, half-standing/half-sitting, awkwardly holding the back of the chair. I finished sitting.

"I'm sorry. No, I've never seen him before. For just a moment, I thought that . . . I'm sorry."

This was so embarrassing. I'd been here less than thirty seconds and had said, "I'm sorry," three times already. I had been distracted. How rude. My hair was a mess. I was hot and sticky. What else could go wrong? And she was so beautiful. So cool and crisp looking. She reached over and her gloved hand touched mine for just a moment. Wow!

"Relax."

The waitress came and took our lunch order. I removed a glove, sipped some water and took several slow deep breaths. Why had I thought of Karen just now? I thought I finally stopped hoping for her. I looked to where the busboy had been, but he was gone. And Karen's gone. Long gone. Long over. Wendy's here.

Wendy watched the waitress walk away. Wendy. Wendy Devlin, banker, age 42. Older woman to my 33. Hot stuff! Was I in lust of a Wendy? Oh, yeah! Wendy had removed a glove also and touched my hand again. I could die right there and be in heaven.

"Thank you for asking me to lunch. I've never been here. It's lovely. So are you."

My cheeks burned again. "Thanks. My hair's a mess. This is my favorite place. I'm glad you came."

I've waited weeks to ask you out.

"How could I not come? You're mother's hero."

"Me?"

"Really. She talks of you all the time. Whenever the memories of her rape get to be too much, she says she thinks of what happened to you. How you were able, as she puts it, 'to kill the fucking bastards.'"

I didn't know what to say. I didn't like to think about what had happened to me. Clare, Wendy's mother, had been raped three years ago and left in a field to die. Her attackers have never been caught. She and I were sister survivors. We met regularly with others to share our stories, our fears, how we live day-to-day with the horrors within us. Clare was a sweet 70-year-old widow who refused to die or be beaten by her trauma. My memories were still fresh and raw, and I thought of Clare and the others as my heroes, my support.

Our tea arrived. Orange pekoe spiced with clove. I poured for each of us.

"Are most of the workers here from England?"

"Pretty much, I think. All the women are from the British Isles, anyway. That busboy must be from the tavern next door helping with the crowd. Phil, Philadelphia Long, the owner, is an Anglophile. She goes to London each year and finds college women willing to come here for a one-year work/study program through Cramer College and hires them for atmosphere. Most go home at the end of their year, but a few, like Elspeth, today's hostess, stay on."

"What a charming idea. What about the cameos? I notice that some wear them and others don't, but the meaning escapes me."

"Availability. The staff knows that most of the women who come here are bent the right way as we like to say." *You're bent the right way, aren't you?* "For those in the know, the cameo says that the wearer is also and wouldn't be offended by being asked out. It prevents awkward moments."

Like this one: not sure which way you're bent—but hoping.

"How nice. Do you date any of them?"

"No."

"Why not?"

"I haven't dated in a really long time." *Until now.*

"Lost love?"

"Something like that." *But I'm hoping for a new one.*

My cell phone rang. *Damn! Why now? Why hadn't I shut it off? This always happens. That's why I hate leaving it on.* It was my lawyer.

"I'm sorry." *There I go again.* "This will just take a moment. This is Rachel."

"Hi, Carmen here. I have another job for you."

"I'm busy at the moment. May I call you back?"

"That's okay. Be at my office tomorrow at nine. This one pays."

"Ten would be better."

"Ten's fine. See you in the morning."

I turned the phone off. I didn't want any more

interruptions. Our lunch arrived. The conversation shifted. Wendy talked about the bank where she worked, and I described my adventure scamming Daniel Morehouse. Safe, inconsequential subjects. Nothing that told me she liked me nor told her how much I wanted to hold her, kiss her, or that I had been longing to be with her ever since Clare introduced us.

She asked me to share a slice of *decadent* chocolate cake for dessert.

"I couldn't possibly eat the whole thing myself."

Did she know she was driving me crazy? I watched the last bite of chocolate disappear between her luscious lips. Mmmmmmmmmmmmm.

She smiled. "I've taken the afternoon off. You promised to show me your Munch."

WENDY STOOD CASUALLY at the bookcase in the living room with her back to me looking at my collection of fantasy and science fiction. She was naked. Her long hair, mussed from our recent lovemaking, streamed down her back. I walked up, put my hands on her hips, slid them around to her belly and pulled her against me, felt her flesh against mine. I buried my face in her hair breathing deeply the faint scent of lavender. She set the book she held on a shelf and pressed her hands over mine. Her hands. Her wonderful hands. Hands that had touched me, teased me, caressed me; pleased me in many, many wonderful ways. I could hardly believe my fortune.

"Is this your gallery of conquests?"

I looked over her shoulder at the two, framed photos.

"Not exactly. 'Lost loves,' as you said earlier. On the left is Karen Tanaka; we were lovers before she left me a year ago."

I stared at Karen smiling impishly back at me. I thought of mistakenly seeing her at Phil's. Karen, if you're not coming back, please don't haunt me.

"The other one is Sarah Hastings. She worked briefly at Phil's Tearoom."

"I thought you didn't date the staff?"

I buried my face in Wendy's hair. "We were going to meet for our first date. She and two men were attacked outside a nightclub back in May. Sarah was killed. You may have read about it?"

"I remember. I'm sorry. Didn't they catch who did it?"

"Yes, but the trials are still pending. One of the killers is in Ohio awaiting extradition, and the bastard, our ex-deputy mayor Vincent Barrow, who set it all up, is out on bail."

"Is her death why you haven't dated?"

I couldn't say anything. Sarah had been the first person I was interested in since Karen left, and she died before we even had a chance to kiss. And now Wendy . . . would anything happen . . .

She twisted around in my arms and held me. Fed me her warmth. We kissed. The tips of our tongues teased one another. Tentative fears disappeared.

Wendy suddenly pulled away. Held me at arm's length with one hand. The sparkle in her green eyes gleamed. She put the back of her other hand to her forehead, turned her face away, and melodramatically sighed.

"You lured me here; seduced me; had your way with me; but, you haven't—haven't shown me the Munch."

I laughed. "Follow me."

I led her to the second master bedroom.

"Linoleum in a bedroom?"

"This was Karen's studio. Linoleum's easier to clean than carpet. There's Edvard Munch's *Madonna*."

I turned on lights and pointed across the bare room to a frameless canvas set on a studio easel in the corner. A spotlight illuminated the painting.

Wendy moved closer. "Oh, my God. It's beautiful."

The painting was the nude torso of a young woman done primarily in browns, ochre and yellow. The curve of a vermilion halo arced behind her flowing black tresses. Her left arm disappeared behind her body as her right one did behind her head. White highlighted chin, nose, cheek, pulling the eye to her face. Her expression was calm repose; waking or falling asleep, her nearly closed eyes invited. Diaphanous blue swirls surrounded her in an air of mystery. Red lips, nipples and navel reflected the color and curve of the halo.

Wendy turned. "When you told Mother and me about the painting, I was expecting a poster, not this. It's wonderful. It's . . . This can't possibly be — "

"No, it's not the one that was stolen last week. It's a copy. Karen painted it years ago at the Munch Museum."

"And she didn't take it when she left you?"

"No. She left in a hurry while I was out of town on a job. She left a lot of stuff behind. Except for these paintings and some furniture, everything's boxed and stored in the closet. I just don't know what to do with it all."

In some ways keep hoping she'll come back for it. For me.

Wendy studied the paintings hung on the white walls. I opened the drapes covering the sliding glass doors to the balcony, and those over the north windows, flooding the room with natural light. Wendy moved with a casual confidence in her nudity. She was as tall as me, five-nine, and athletically trim. Her breasts were a wonderfully sized B cup. A ragged appendectomy scar added to her beauty instead of detracting. Karen would have loved painting— Stop it! Stop right now! I don't need another *ménage*. I took a deep breath and leaned against the wall.

Wendy stood before a small seascape not much larger than a sheet of paper of a dark open sailboat pulling strongly through the waves, aimed at the moon. Sky and sea shimmered through thick paint and multiple glazes; so different from the thin washes of the *Madonna*.

"I think I remember this, from art history, years ago."

"Another copy Karen painted: *Toilers of the Sea* by Albert Pinkham Ryder. The rest are originals."

"This is unbelievable. It's like a gallery, a museum."

There were seven of Karen's original paintings, all of them large; maybe that was why she left them behind. She was fascinated by Munch and Ryder; often called them expressionistic visionaries and described her own work as a fusion of the two. It was easy, even for a non-artist like me, to see their influence. Wendy came and looked at the large figure painting beside me. She looked back at the *Madonna*. The pose and free-flowing style were quite similar—even to the halo—while Ryder-like thick, shimmering glazes dominated.

"This is you."

"'Fraid so."

"Your hair was long and blonde. Why did you cut it?"

"Pissed at Karen for leaving. She liked it long. Dumb reason. Now I'm growing it back."

Wendy reached out and ran her fingers through my hair. "I like the color." She pulled my face to hers.

AT 3:00 AM, I lay curled in bed sipping a glass of Glenfiddich. I pulled a pillow to me. It faintly held Wendy's scent from the afternoon. The thought of our second lovemaking on the cool linoleum in Karen's studio made me quiver. I wished again that Wendy had stayed, that she were here now curled next to me. What happened between us was more than sudden lust; it had to be.

I put my glass on the nightstand; my cell phone lay there, tempting me. I reached for it and stopped.

You can't be serious?

I rolled over and stared at the ceiling. Why not?

Because today was real, not a fantasy. That's why not. Why spoil it?

I looked at the phone. That's real too.

That's an obsession. It's nutty.

So is lying here arguing with myself.

What would Wendy say?

I don't know. How do I explain obsession?

I picked up the phone and speed-dialed. Margo Lane answered on the second ring. There was no preamble, no greeting. I didn't need to speak. I never speak. He knew who it was. We both knew why we continued to play this bizarre game: him speaking, me listening. In so many ways, we were incompatible. He was a transvestite who prefers men. I prefer women. This, this was ours alone. No touching, but a deeper sensation than anything either of us ever knew.

It started when we first met at Miss Kitty's Kathouse Kabaret. Margo was the club manager and I was investigating the attacks on the club's gay performers. Inadvertently, we discovered his voice could drop to a deep pitch that somehow aroused me beyond belief. I needed to know at the time if it were only a fluke — a one-time thing — and called him late that first night to hear it again, to see if it were real. It was. It became my obsession and has gotten me through many rough times and nights. When he discovered the power his voice had over a single human being — even if it were a woman, and for some reason it only affects me — it became his obsession as well.

Margo's voice dropped to that wonderfully deep low rumble, the vibes drilling into the center of my being. It's so difficult to explain, to understand. A sound system set for maximum bass, maximum vibration, multiplied a hundred thousand times comes close.

To me, it never matters what he says; only that he keep speaking. This isn't phone sex in the usual sense; no pornographic detail of what goes where, who does what, no heavy breathing. The timbre of his voice, not the words, excites me. Yet he strives to fill me with exotic words. Tonight, his words . . .

"My sweetest Lesbia, let us live and love, and though the sager sort our deeds reprove . . ."

Three

Tᴜᴇsᴅᴀʏ ᴍᴏʀɴɪɴɢ I ʙᴏᴜɴᴄᴇᴅ into the law offices of Andrews and Pfeiffer at five of ten. Jon, the receptionist, returned my buoyant smile.

"You're looking unusually chipper. I'll let Ms. Andrews know you're here."

Just then, my lawyer, Carmen Andrews, came down the hall.

"Hi, Rachel. Prompt as usual. You look happy."

"Why not? It's a beautiful morning. And you said you had a job that paid. I hope that means money in my pocket, not just paying back what I still owe you."

"Your bill's dwindling; don't worry about it."

"I have to worry. These past three months have been tight. My reserves are down and the 'boob fund' is zilch. Process serving and background checks don't pay enough."

"Whose fault is that?"

"You sound like my doctor."

"Well, this involves serving papers, but first you have to find the guy. So this is a full-pay gig. My client *finally* filed for divorce yesterday, but her husband is missing. She's in my office now, if you think you're ready to handle it. Jon, no disturbances until we're through."

Carmen and my psychiatrist, Dr. Natalie Howard, were right. I was avoiding real work, anything beyond the safe predictable pale. I lost a potential lover; I was tortured and raped; I killed people. I lost a lot of myself and the healing was taking longer than I thought or hoped. But now I had Wendy. Wendy, Wendy, Wendy.

The woman standing at the window held the curtain back and stared out. The view from Carmen's office is not that exciting. It looks out on an alley and dumpsters for a Chinese restaurant.

"Louise," Carmen said, "this is Rachel Cord, the investigator we talked about. Rachel, this is Louise Carter."

"How do you do?"

Louise Carter gave me a tight smile and nodded. Her eyes were red. She held her black purse tight to her body. She was overweight, but attractive, about 30. Her short dark hair was styled. She wore a black jacket and skirt with a gray blouse. Too drab and dark for the weather. She looked more like a recent widow than a woman seeking a divorce.

Carmen sat at her desk; Louise Carter and I sat in the leather bound chairs facing it.

"Louise's husband left Friday night for a weekend with a friend of his. He does this too often, which is one of myriad reasons for the divorce. This was the first time though he didn't come home Sunday evening. Louise called me and said she had had enough. I filed the papers for her first thing yesterday. We spoke again in the early afternoon; Jerry hadn't returned, and he missed two scheduled business appointments. He never misses appointments. That's when I called you. He's still missing."

"Ms. Carter, do you know this friend of his?"

"Call me Louise, please. Yes, Stan is an old friend of Jerry's. He was best man at our wedding. They grew up together. When Jerry didn't come home on time, I called his cell phone but all I got was voicemail. Then I called Stan. No one answered there either. I left a message, but no one called back. That's when I called Carmen. I was angry. When Jerry missed his appointments, I began to worry. I tried calling him and Stan again, but still no answers."

"What does your husband do?"

"He's a computer programmer and design consultant. He has his own business. He works from home."

"Has he done anything like this before?"

"Never."

"Have you called the hospitals? There may have been an accident."

"No. I was afraid to."

"How about the police? Have you reported him missing?"

"No. Jerry wouldn't like that."

This was strange. I looked at Carmen. Carmen leaned forward.

"Louise and her husband are very private people. We'd like you to look into this first. If it becomes necessary to contact the authorities, that's something to discuss later."

Something was rotten and this wasn't Denmark.

"Louise, how long have you been married?"

"Four years."

"Children?"

"Three. Two boys, one girl. The youngest is eight months."

I hoped the boys were twins. That's a lot of time being pregnant. I glanced at her feet. Sensible shoes, black flats. She wasn't barefoot.

"How old is your husband?"

"Twenty-seven."

"What's his full name?

"Jerome Albert Carter."

"And his friend Stan?"

"Kenneth Wayne Stanley."

The name gave me pause. I didn't know him and had never heard his name before. It was the "Wayne" middle name that got to me. I had read recently one of those oddities in life features in the newspaper. It was a list of half-a-dozen or more people whose middle name was Wayne and who had been arrested and charged with or convicted of murder this summer; and that's just recently. They brought back memories of the biggest hoodoo of my youth, John Wayne Gacy.

It was Christmas time, when I was six or seven, and I watched news reports that my parents didn't know I was seeing of all those bodies being taken from that home near Chicago—which even that young I knew was only a few hours drive from our home—and the pictures of the Clown Man who was responsible for all of the deaths. It didn't register, or matter, that all of those dead people were young men; I thought the Clown Man was going to come get me too. He gave me nightmares for years. The mere sight of a clown could make me pee my pants. I even stopped watching Bozo on TV. Years later, that TV movie with Brian Dennehy didn't help either. My fear of clowns isn't that bad any longer, but I don't go to circuses or McDonalds. What was I getting myself into?

"Where does Mr. Stanley live?"

"Across the river. Just outside of town."

Across the river. I looked again at Carmen. She had on her neutral court face. Didn't say anything. Just handed me a check that lay on the desk. It was Louise's and made out to me for $1,000. It wouldn't fill the bank, but it would make the first-of-the-month bills easier to pay. For $1,000, Louise could buy 10 hours of my time and either resolution or a progress report. She'd have to decide then if she wanted me to continue.

I used to average three cases a month at $100 an hour, which includes most expenses, with a nonrefundable grand up front. Sometimes I'd get lucky and close a case in less than 10 hours; most take longer. My average was 34 hours. These were not contiguous hours, of course. Most investigation involves an hour or two of action and a lot of waiting for information to come back. The in-between you fill with other work. Process serving and background checks at a set fee help fill in the gaps. I wasn't getting rich—seems like two-thirds goes to expenses and taxes, and my condo mortgage isn't small—but I was getting ahead and my boob reduction fund had been filling nicely.

Then I got hurt. Badly. Now the in-between was all I was doing and it was barely paying the bills, and the boob money went for medical bills my insurance didn't cover instead of the breast reduction I craved. I was also doing little jobs *gratis* for Carmen, to pay off legal work she had done for me. I didn't want to do this—especially going across the river again. It was another state and I wasn't licensed there. Bad things happened across the river. Carmen knew this but didn't say anything. I wanted to yell at her. Scream, "No way! Not again!" But I didn't. I needed the money.

Louise answered more questions. We arranged to meet later at her house so I could get a picture of her husband and a look at his office.

I left Carmen's feeling uneasy and still a bit angry. I wanted to go back in and say I couldn't do it. Give the check back. I wasn't sure if my uneasiness was because of the case itself or just nervousness about getting back to real work. Or the thought of going back across the river.

Three months ago I went across the river looking for a runaway teenager. I had no official standing over there. My state doesn't license PIs, and I wasn't licensed there either. That didn't stop me then. I found the girl, Linda Miller, drugged and imprisoned. Before I could free her, I was brutally beaten, raped and nearly killed by Gwen Archer and her accomplice Calvin Tierney. They were running a child pornography and prostitution racket, and I was interfering. As Wendy's mother said, I "killed the fucking bastards." Even so, flashbacks could still make me pee myself.

A state attorney over there had wanted me charged with murder. Luckily, when publicity about the takedown of the porno ring got out, and bodies of lost teens were found buried on Tierney's land, charges against me were eventually dropped; even the ones for practicing without a license. But it was made abundantly clear that my presence was strictly *persona non grata*. I haven't been back; didn't want to go back; but for $1,000, I was.

The memory was stifling. I needed some positive energy. I called Wendy at her bank. Thinking of her gave me a thrill.

"Hi, this is Rachel. I'm downtown. Are you free for lunch?"

Please. Please.

"I'd love to, but sorry, not today. Too many meetings."

"Darn. I wanted to see you."

"How about dinner?"

Yes!

"I'd like that. When and where?"

"How about I pick you up at seven? Dress casual. Do you like spicy?"

I like you.

"Spicy, but not necessarily hot, if you know what I mean."

"I understand. Good. This will give me a chance to thank you for yesterday's lunch."

"You thanked me quite nicely already."

"That was pleasure, not thanks."

"It was wonderful."

"I would hope so. You were on top. My butt is still cold from that linoleum."

My cheeks burned. She chuckled. Could anyone at the bank overhear what she was saying?

"It was wonderful," she agreed. "I'm glad you want to see me again, because I want to see you too. Got to get back to work. See you tonight."

See me tonight! Hal-le-lu-jah! Hal-le-lu-jah! Hallelujah, Hallelujah. Haaaa-le-luu-jaaah! Hal —

A lady sitting at the bus stop across the street stared at

me. She wasn't disapproving or smiling. Maybe she was nearsighted, but I stopped dancing about. Behind her was Uni-Cuts offering haircuts for $6. Maybe a light trim and shaping would control my mop; my do-it-yourself methods weren't working. Next door was Peaches Beauty Therapy offering Brazilian wax specials. I smiled as I crossed the street and thought of a bit of a surprise for Wendy.

Leaving Peaches, where Barb the owner did an awesome job on my surprise, I went home, straightened the condo and changed the sheets; spent an hour picking something casual to wear for dinner; then drove to my office to run a computer check on Jerome Carter and Kenneth Wayne Stanley before going to the Carter house. For $50 a month and a dollar a report, you can find out nearly anything on anyone.

Neither had any arrests or convictions. Both were born and raised across the river and attended Cramer College here. Carter had a BS and an MS in computer science. Stanley had a BS in political science. Stanley still lived across the river at a rural box number address. Carter had the typical half dozen credit cards and several store revolving accounts. Most were nearly maxed out, but payments were current. Curiously, Stanley had no credit history. I also called area hospitals on both sides of the river. No help there.

At 3:55, I parked in front of the Carter house in Northside Village. It was a typical ranch-style with a converted two-car garage. There was a gray Buick Park Avenue in the driveway.

A heavyset Hispanic woman answered the door. She led me to the kitchen where Louise and a three-year-old boy were attempting handmade tortillas. There was a stack of them on a plate next to a flatiron hot griddle. Something was simmering on the stove in cast-iron pots. The smells of cumin, cilantro and cinnamon made my mouth water. Louise cleaned her hands on her apron as I entered.

"I forgot you were coming. Stan, this is Miss Cord. This is our eldest, Kenneth Stanley Carter. He's named after Jerry's friend. Juanita, would you watch him, please? Miss Cord and I have some business to discuss."

"*Si, Senora.*"

"Do you know where my daddy is?"

Stan looked right at me. He had flour on his cheek.

"No, I don't. But I will try to find him."

"Tell him we made tortillas."

"Okay. I will."

Louise led me back through the house. She seemed more relaxed and in control in her home. In a playpen I had missed on the way in, a little girl was absorbed with her stuffed animals.

"That's Felicia." Louise said quietly. "Wayne is asleep in the nursery."

We went into what had been the garage. It had been divided into a laundry/work/storage area and an office.

"The children aren't allowed in here." Louise whispered.

She hesitated before unlocking the office door. Maybe the children weren't the only ones not allowed in there.

"I still haven't heard anything from Jerry or Stan."

"I checked area hospitals. They aren't there either, and there have been no John Does admitted. You said earlier that Jerry and Stanley grew up together. Does Jerry still have family in the area?"

"No. Jerry never knew his father. He died when Jerry was an infant. Felicia, Jerry's mom, never remarried. She moved to Florida when Jerry was in college."

Three computers were set up along one wall on a continuous countertop. One was running, but the screen was blank. Along a second wall were bookcases filled with various computer books and dozens of black binders. Several old computers were displayed like artifacts. There was an original Macintosh and one I had never heard of, a LISA. There was also a VIC-10. One of my brothers had had one. You used a TV as your monitor. What Wally really wanted back then was a Commador-64 that had color.

Carter's desk looked out over the driveway, a four-drawer filing cabinet filled one corner, and there were several chairs. A wastebasket with a shredder mounted on top was empty beside the desk. The office had its own exit.

Lined up on the desk like a squad of soldiers were a telephone; a photograph of two men smiling and holding freshly caught fish; a desk calendar opened to Monday, August 30; and studio photographs of each child. There was no photograph of Louise. The desk blotter was clean, no stains, no doodles. There were no pens or pencils or notepad or paperclips or stickies or anything else. There was barely a layer of dust on the mahogany surface from four days' nonuse. It was beyond neat.

I looked around the room again. Everything was "Dress Right, Dress" as we would have said in the Army, squared up and face forward. Ready for inspection. The only things casual in the whole room were the two men in the photograph on the desk. Did someone actually work here?

"Louise, do you come in here often?"

"No. Jerry likes his privacy. I only came in yesterday because of the clients who showed up when Jerry wasn't here."

"Does the housekeeper clean in here?"

"No. Jerry does it. As I said, he likes his privacy."

"Did you change the calendar?"

"No. It was like that."

Carter must have done it before he left on Friday. He knew he had appointments. Louise must be as frustrated as I was when Karen left.

"Who pays the bills?"

I tried the central drawer on the desk. It was locked.

"Jerry does."

"Any financial problems?"

The other drawers were also locked although there were no visible keyholes.

"Not that I'm aware of. Our joint account is fine. I'm sure that Jerry's business account is also. We never receive late notices. Jerry would never allow that to happen. He pays everything promptly."

I'll bet he does. The filing cabinet was locked, also. I walked over to the running computer and pressed the "Return" key. The screen lit and a message read, "Enter password." On a whim, I typed in S-T-A-N and pressed "Return."

"Access denied. Enter password."

I looked around the room trying to think of what Carter might use as a password. I looked at the old computers. I typed in L-I-S-A.

"Access denied. Enter password."

I'm not a computer geek, nor a psychologist. I had no idea what would open Carter's computer. I tried O-P-E-N, L-O-U-I-S-E, F-E-L-I-C-I-A and J-U-N-I-O-R. As a last attempt, I entered S-E-S-A-M-E. That didn't work either.

"I don't suppose you know his password?"

"No. Jerry —"

"Wouldn't like that, I know."

I turned to face her. Her eyes were watering as she tightly pressed her lips together.

"I'm sorry. I shouldn't have said that. Your husband is missing and you're worried. I had no reason to be flip."

"Jerry is very . . . orderly. He likes things . . . neat. We . . ."

Tears began rolling down her cheeks. I put my arms around her and held her. She buried her face in my bosom and cried. There was a bit of flour in her hair. What does Jerry think of his not so orderly family?

Louise moved away. "I'm sorry. I love my husband, but things have really gotten out of hand. That's why the divorce. And now this. It's so unlike Jerry. He's always so methodical and organized. He is never late. I'm really worried. I don't want to scare the children. I just don't know what to do."

Louise slumped into one of the chairs. She almost bounced right up again, afraid to be sitting in Jerry's domain. She settled.

"The first thing to do is see if we can find him. Does he keep the checkbook and bills in the desk?"

"Yes. He gives me the bills to mail when they're ready to go out."

"This desk is beautiful. I'd hate to ruin it. You wouldn't know where he keeps the key, would you?"

She turned pale. "Jerry wouldn't—" She stopped; took a deep breath. "It may be in his dresser. He doesn't take anything he doesn't need with him when he goes out."

"Let's go see."

Her eyes widened; then she nodded.

Good for you. There's hope for you yet.

The bedroom was just as neat as Carter's office. The tops of both dressers were cleared except for a family portrait on Louise's. The king-sized bed had a solid blue bedspread pulled smoothly. I could picture tight hospital corners on the sheets and blanket. Would my old drill sergeant be able to bounce a quarter off the spread? Carter had been gone four days and Louise still made the bed to his liking. Did these two really make babies in this bed?

The key to Carter's desk was in the top drawer of the dresser along with cufflinks and tie clasps. I quickly rifled through the other drawers to see if there were anything hidden. There wasn't. Except that he rolled his socks and undershorts—my drill sergeant would have been so proud—and everything was too neat, I didn't find anything of interest. Louise seemed agitated by my looking but didn't say anything.

We went back to the office. The center desk drawer contained a notepad, a Cross fountain pen and mechanical pencil. The top page of the pad was blank. Even holding it to the light revealed no impressions from previous pages. Carter must tear off each page before using it. I didn't think he was the type to waste extra pages. Apparently he shredded everything.

Opening the center drawer released the other locks. I

found the checkbooks and file folders for each credit card and bill. The checkbooks had healthy balances and the registers were filled in meticulously. There didn't seem to be any unusual withdrawals. The file folders were thick. There was several years' worth of statements. My accountant would be ecstatic. I have two credit cards: one for business, one personal. Sometimes I mix them up. I toss all of my receipts together into a shoebox.

A quick scan told me which credit card Carter used on his weekend jaunts. It was used every Sunday for most of the past year and a half at the same convenience store across the river. Before that, it was used at the same spot once or twice a month.

"I don't mean to be personal, but when did you start thinking your marriage was falling apart?"

"While I was pregnant with Wayne. Jerry began spending every weekend with Stan. The past few months he's been neglecting the children as well as me. Which wasn't like him. He's a good father. I told Carmen about it back in March. She told me then to get a divorce. Carmen and I have been friends since high school."

"Could your husband be having an affair and using his friend as cover?"

"I . . . I don't know. I don't think so. Wouldn't a wife know?"

"Not necessarily."

"Oh. Is that what happened, do you think? He's run off with another woman?"

"I won't know until I find him. Do you work?"

"Not since I first got pregnant. The children are too young for me to be away, I think. Once they're all in school, I'll find work."

Good luck. I looked again at the photograph of the two fishermen. They were unshaven with windblown hair and wearing checked flannel shirts. They had an arm around each other and held their catches high with their other hands. It was a casual, carefree moment that didn't square with what I perceived as a controlling, uptight individual.

"The men in this picture, is this your husband and his friend?"

"Yes. Jerry's on the left. That was taken in the fall shortly before Jerry and I married."

"May I take it?"

"I have a more recent photo for you."

"That will be fine."

Four

WENDY SNUGGLED AGAINST me in bed, her thigh pressed between my legs, her head on my breast, my arms around her. Her hair smelled erotically of curry and other spices from the small Indian restaurant where we had dinner. It had been a wonderful evening of fascinating tastes and piquant learning of each other.

Between the samosas and dal, the channa masala and aloo poshto, Goanese vegetable curry, several breads, and sweet mango lassi for dessert, we talked.

Wendy told me about her marriage to a grad student her last semester of college. It lasted three turbulent years.

"Luckily, there were no children; it was still a messy divorce. I reverted to my maiden name afterwards."

There were brief relationships with other men, but nothing permanent. At 29, Wendy met her life partner, Nancy Witford.

"She was my first—and only—true love. She talked me into applying to Wharton and getting my MBA and PhD."

Nancy died five years ago from aggressive pancreatic cancer. When Clare was raped, Wendy moved home. Since Nancy's death, she dated some but had not had another sexual relationship, until now.

I told her about growing up in small-town Iowa with three older brothers; my first lesbian experience at 15 with my best friend, Betty Jean Cooper; how difficult it was to keep that relationship, and a couple later ones, hidden from disapproving family and neighbors in such a small community; how I ran away at 18 and joined the Army.

"I had to keep what I was hidden there too, but it got me out of Iowa and gave me a lot of freedom. Actually, there were a lot of us who served, and are serving, in our country's uniforms."

I told her more about Karen: how we met, fell in love; how Karen talked me into buying such a large condo; how hurt I was when she left without a word, and sent my letters back unopened when I'd traced her to Florida.

We returned to my condo and I gave Wendy a more complete tour than her previous visit.

"There are three bedrooms, three baths, kitchen with breakfast bar opening to the living room that I also use for dining; a separate dining room that was Karen's office; the furniture's still there, but I've boxed her stuff; and a balcony that goes the whole width looking out over the river."

"It's much larger than I thought. I think I'd get lost living here alone."

"It's lonely sometimes."

"It must have been expensive."

"More than I wanted to spend. Karen convinced me I could handle it with her paying half."

Now is another question.

"Is she half-owner?"

"No. I got a VA loan for it, so it's only in my name. Karen insisted. Maybe she knew then that she was leaving someday."

"She was a fool for leaving you. It must be difficult without her paying a share any longer."

"I'm managing." So far.

"You could re-finance. Rates are way down. That would

lower your payments. I could look into that, if you'd like."

"Thanks. That's a good idea."

We ended up back in the studio. Wendy again admired the *Madonna,* and the portrait of me.

"I like this one better."

Wendy glanced down at the floor, then at me. She smiled mischievously and waggled her eyebrows in what I thought of as a Groucho Marx leer. I blushed, but that didn't stop us from pulling each other's clothes off and making love — again — on the linoleum. She claimed dibs for being on top. God! It *was* cold on the butt.

We lay comfortably later curled in bed. I breathed in Wendy's scents. Held her closer. She rubbed her face against my breast and caressed my other one.

"Your breasts are like pillows."

I tensed.

She raised her head. "What's wrong? What did I say?"

I hugged her. "Nothing. Karen used to say something like that. Called me her *'makura makura,'* her 'pillow pillow' girl."

"Sorry."

"No need to be."

But will you like my breasts when they're smaller? Will you still like me? I certainly hope so.

Wendy rose up, brought her lips to mine, then slid down the bed throwing the covers off. A fingernail traced my newly modified and heart-shaped pubic patch sending shivers through me.

"This was a sweet surprise."

A surprise to me too considering the last time my pubic hair was removed was by Gwen Archer with a pair of pliers. Maybe I was finally healing.

"I'm glad you like it."

"I do. It's sweet and *so* red. And to think, Valentine's Day is still six months away."

Wendy nuzzled me to show just how sweet she thought it was. Oh, boy!

I woke later and the space beside me was empty. Wendy's clothes still hung on hangars from the closet door. The bathroom door was open but the room was dark. Through the open bedroom door reflected light from somewhere lit the living room.

I found Wendy sitting in Karen's studio. She had brought a chair in from the balcony. All of the lights were on. She was wrapped in my white terry robe. She held the photograph of Karen from the bookcase.

"What are you doing in here?"

"Trying to understand why she left you?"

I leaned against the doorway. "Lots of luck. I never figured it out. I've finally just accepted it."

Wendy looked at the photo. "Did you take this picture?"

"Yes. We had a day on the river and were having a very good time. She was always an imp, and I thought that picture captured it."

Wendy got up and walked around the room studying the paintings.

"There's a deep passion in her paintings. And in her expression in this photo, so full of fun." She turned toward me. "I can't believe this woman just up and left you."

"Me either. But she did. If she hadn't, you probably wouldn't be here."

"True." Wendy came and put her arms around me. "Maybe I'm afraid she'll come back."

Me too.

Five

WENDY SIPPED HER COFFEE as I lay my bag on the counter. She was dressed and ready to leave for work. She seemed comfortable, right at home. I liked that. It'd been a long time since sharing breakfast chores. This was nice. I could see us . . . What am I thinking? This was too new — too soon — to even think of us as a couple. Would she even consider moving —

"What?"

"I asked, 'will you be gone all day?'"

"Most likely."

"Too bad. I have time today for a quick . . . lunch."

She waggled her eyebrows in that Groucho Marx way again.

I felt the blush coming and opened my shoulder bag quickly to distract me. I breathed slowly and deeply as I double-checked that I had the photo Louise gave me. The studio portrait was more how I pictured Carter than the casual fisherman: serious, clean-shaven, not a hair out of place, regulation tie perfectly knotted, crisp white shirt and dark-blue coat. I also had Stanley's address, the address of the convenience store where Carter used his credit card so often, a map, and the divorce papers if I found Carter. Feeling calmer, I looked at Wendy.

"Can I call you tonight? Will you be home?"

"Yes, please do. Do you carry a gun?"

"Not for something like this. Besides, my carry permit isn't valid across the river. I'm not licensed to practice over there either, but that shouldn't be a problem. This is just a simple find and deliver. Will Clare worry that you stayed out all night?"

"Of course not. I'm a big girl. And so is she. She'll just hope I had a good time."

Did you?

Wendy smiled and came over to me.

"To answer your unasked question, yes, I did." She kissed me. "Be careful today."

THE SUN BEAT DOWN as I huddled against the rough logs of the garage. Nightmares flooded my mind, my body. I had no control. The torture and rape I endured months ago engulfed me, threatening to destroy me again. I relived every moment, every pain, every humiliation. And relived the satisfaction that surged through me when I put two bullets into Gwen Archer and placed the barrel of my gun to Calvin Tierney's left eye and pulled the trigger.

I tried to stand—my legs and arms rigid and achy—wobbled to my feet. My pants were wet. I had peed myself. I checked to see if I had done worse. It wouldn't have been the first time. I breathed slowly, letting the nightmares dissipate, remembering where I was and why.

I wanted to run away, hide. Wanted to be home curled in with Wendy or be with one of my survivor friends. I didn't want to face another nightmare but had no choice. I eased into the garage. The smell wasn't as bad; fresh air flowed through the open garage door. The room was still hot, but not unbearable. I moved to the naked body on the floor.

It was a man and he was alive. He had uncurled since I first saw him. His skin was warm and slick with sweat. I felt a slow, steady pulse, and he was breathing shallowly. A chain ran around his middle with wrist shackles loosely attached to it. An eight-foot chain was attached at his back and to a metal ring in the center of the mat attached to the floor. His head, except for his mouth and nose, was covered in a leather hood. There were no eyeholes.

I removed the hood. It was Jerome Carter. He had several days beard growth. Removing the hood roused him.

"S-S-Sta," he gasped. "Where have—"

"I'm not Stan. Lie still. I'll get help."

"N-N-No. Water. Please."

I went to the sink and filled a glass with water. I held him up. He reeked of stale sweat and dried urine. He was trying to focus, wondering who I was. He sipped the water. He drank the whole glass. I refilled it. He slowly drank all of it.

"You need help, Mr. Carter. You should be in the hospital. The sheriff needs to find who did this to you."

Was it Kenneth Wayne Stanley?

"N-N-No. Please. D-Don't." His voice was still weak. "You don't . . . don't understand. It was a game. Please. Don't call anyone."

A game? I looked around. There were two dog bowls on the floor. One still held a trace of what I thought was granola. The other was empty. It had probably contained water. When did it run out? There was a camp toilet, a low stool with a plastic bag attached beneath it. It had been used. How had he managed that chained and sightless? What the hell kind of game was this?

Carter tried to get up. "Please. I can explain. Just help me. Don't call anyone. That's all I ask. Please."

I thought he needed more help than I could offer, but an EMT call would probably bring the police also. I wasn't ready to make explanations of why I was on this side of the river again. I finally nodded. He pointed as best he could.

"There are keys hanging by the door."

Carter sat at the kitchen table eating the eggs and toast I made. I sat drinking coffee. He looked and smelled a lot better. I had helped him shower and dress. It had been hard getting him into the house. I wore an oversized T-shirt and a man's jeans while my own clothes washed. They stank from contact with Carter and my own accident. Helping him had helped rebury my flashback. I was still shaken but back in control. Carter stared at his plate, avoiding eye contact.

"Who are you? How did you find me?"

"My name is Rachel Cord. I'm a private investigator. Your wife hired me to find you when you didn't come home. I'm also supposed to deliver this." I slid the envelope across the table to him. "Your wife is getting a divorce."

He touched the envelope but didn't pick it up. He still didn't look at me.

"Finding me like that must have been pretty disgusting."

To say the least.

"You said you had an explanation."

"What's today?"

"Wednesday, September first."

"Where's Stan?"

"I don't know. No one else is here. Yours is the only car here. I presume he left in his."

"Something must have happened to him. Stan wouldn't leave me like that."

"I checked hospitals when your wife said she couldn't reach either of you. He hasn't been admitted anywhere. Of course, it's possible he's been arrested for something. I haven't contacted the police." Yet.

"Stan wouldn't get arrested. He doesn't even get traffic tickets. Despite what you've seen or may think, Stan and I are law-abiding citizens."

I looked around the kitchen. Everything was neat except for the small mess I made making breakfast. I remembered the parts of the house I had seen: the living room, bedroom, bathroom, laundry room. Everything had been put away, straightened. The whole house was like Carter's office.

Carter got up taking his plate and glass and the plate I

had used for the toast to the sink. He carefully washed the items before putting them in the dishwasher. He cleaned the skillet and set it in the oven. He wiped up crumbs and spatters of grease. He moved slowly and hesitantly. He looked pale, but it was hard to imagine this tidy, neatly dressed man as the dehydrated, foul mess I had found little more than two hours ago. As he worked, he talked.

"Something must have happened to Stan. I know it. Nothing would keep him away this long. We've been friends since grade school. He wouldn't do this to me. He wouldn't have left Amber with no food."

"Mr. Carter, I find it hard to balance what you're telling me with how I found you."

"I can imagine. That scene is so unlike the rest of my life, or Stan's. Call it, 'our escape valve.' It really was a game. A bizarre game, but a game nonetheless. It's been going on a long time. These last few months, it's getting even—"

"Mr. Carter. Before you go any further, I should warn you that anything you say I am obligated to reveal to my client and to her attorney."

"Thanks for the warning. But something happened to Stan. It's been . . . four days, you say? I need to find him. Will you help me find him?"

"I work for your wife. It would be a conflict of interest to work for you too."

Carter sat down. "How much is she paying you? What were the arrangements?"

"I was paid to find you and serve you with those papers. How much I'm paid is between my client and me."

Carter picked up the envelope. Then he looked at me again.

"You found me. You delivered this. Your job's done. Now let me hire you. I'll pay you twice what my wife was paying."

It was tempting. I could really use the money. But it meant I'd spend more time on this side of the river. How long before I had to let the authorities know I was here? What would they say?

"Please. I don't know where else to turn. You found me in the garage—by the way, thanks—but I don't know how to explain this situation to the police."

Me either. And I certainly didn't want to. Common sense told me not to do it, but . . .

"We'll worry about the police if we need to. I won't charge you double. I get $100 an hour, plus any unusual expenses, and I get a thousand up front that's nonrefundable. But first, I need to close out this assignment."

He looked relieved for the first time. I pulled my cell phone from my shoulder bag and turned it on.

"Louise? This is Rachel. I found your husband. He's okay."

"Are you sure he's all right? Where is he? Why didn't he come home? Can I talk to him?"

"He's fine. I found him at Stanley's. Things were complicated. He was . . . tied up and couldn't get home. The details will be in my report. Here. Talk to him."

I held out the phone. Carter shook his head. I continued to hold it out to him. We could hear Louise's tinny voice saying, "Jerry? Jerry? Are you there? Speak to me."

"If you want me to work for you, talk to her."

Carter took the phone. I left the room.

He found me sitting in the enclosed porch with Amber on my lap. He returned my phone and sat in one of the wicker chairs. I turned the phone off and returned it to my bag.

"Do you have to tell my wife how you found me? About the details, I mean?"

"I was working for her. She's entitled to know everything that I do and find. Please understand that if you intend to contest the divorce, everything you tell me about you and Stanley could end up in testimony. There's no attorney/client privilege here. I don't enjoy that privilege on my own. You might want to reconsider hiring me. There are other investigators."

"That's all right. I should have expected this was going to happen someday. I told Louise I would be home soon. I'll tell her everything then. This is going to hurt her. I never intended to hurt her."

Carter handed me a check for $1,000. He leaned forward staring out the window, looking past the garage and across the meadow at the weathered barn. I didn't prod or ask questions. I waited until he was ready. This had to be difficult for him. He kept rubbing his hands together like he was washing them, trying to get them clean.

"It started down there." His voice was soft, reminiscent. "Stan and I were eleven, maybe twelve; in sixth or seventh grade, anyway. I don't remember for sure. We built a treehouse in the woods behind the barn. It's still there. We played pirates and Viking warriors. Beating on each other with swords made of rolled up newspapers and cardboard shields. We built a submarine in the meadow. It was pasture then; they had some horses. We made a periscope from a cardboard carpet core and two mirrors. Two young boys hauling used lumber from the barn, scavenging nails. We made torpedo tubes from some old metal tanks we cut open with hacksaws, and we used cut up inner tubes to launch our torpedoes, which were more carpet cores. We'd see whose torpedo could go the farthest. We lived in our imaginations.

"Somewhere we found some girlie magazines and a porno book. We'd read them in our hideaway. Told dirty jokes. Dry humped, taking turns pretending to be the girl. Did 'circle jerk' stuff. I was circumcised, Stan wasn't. Stan was the first to actually come. Then one day his sister caught us.

"Danny was three years older than Stan. Her name was Dana, but the family called her Danny. She came down to get us for supper. We didn't hear her. We were on our knees, with our pants down, masturbating, trying to see who would come first on a magazine centerfold on the ground between us. She scared the hell out of us. We begged and pleaded for her not to tell on us. Said we'd do anything she asked.

"That was probably a mistake. I don't know. But it was a big influence on how Stan and I developed. She made us finish what we were doing while she watched. Then she had us lick our come off the page, or she'd tell. I remember gagging that first time. It smelled a little like bleach.

"Whether the next two years were heaven or hell, I don't know. Danny had complete control, and she enjoyed using it. Every time we did her bidding, no matter how bizarre or painful, there'd be a sexual reward. She also punished us. It was exciting and forbidden, and, maybe, a bit scary. Maybe that's why we kept doing whatever she wanted."

Carter paused and sat back. He still looked out across the meadow, his gaze unfocused.

"Danny ran away when she was seventeen. By then, Stan and I were hooked on each other and into kinky stuff. We continued together right through college. There would be an occasional girlfriend, or boyfriend, but it was what we experienced together that gave us our most pleasure. You probably don't understand that kind of obsession."

I wouldn't say that.

"Anyway, Stan's parents were killed in a car accident coming to see us graduate at Cramer College. Stan was devastated. He'd only gone to college to please them and be with me. He inherited everything. Danny had been cut out of the will after she ran away. Stan came back here while I stayed to work on my masters. That's when I met Louise.

"I fell in love with her. With Stan gone, I thought I could have a normal life. It didn't work out that way. I still saw Stan once or twice a month. Then Louise got pregnant and we married. She's a wonderful mother, but pregnancy is hard on her. She'd have morning sickness, and gain too much weight. Weight that became harder to lose after each child. And then there was all that baby stuff. It was gross. Raising children wasn't any fun. Louise thrives on it, but the disorder and unpredictability upsets me.

"I was always fairly neat, but I withdrew into myself and my orderly world. Concentrated on business. It was unfair to Louise. Unfair to my kids. My only outlet was the occasional weekend with Stan. Then came the third pregnancy. I wanted Louise to get an abortion, but I couldn't tell her that. That's when I started seeing Stan every week. The more controlled my life with Louise, the more depraved my time with Stan. I made him punish me for the lie I was living. How you found me was part of that."

Tears welled in Carter's eyes. He was drained. We sat without speaking for several minutes. He turned to me.

"What happened to Stan? Where is he?"

Six

CARTER AND I WENT through the house. I suggested starting with Stanley's message machine.

"You have nine messages." "Stan? This is Gilmore. Where the hell are you? Cameron just called saying you didn't open up this morning. You better be at work." "Saturday, 9:13 AM." "Hey, Stan? Pick up. Mr. Gilmore's hoppin' mad. Said you better have a good excuse for missing work. Gimme a call." "Saturday, 11:43 AM." "This is Louise Carter. Is Jerry still with you? He hasn't come home. Is everything all right? Please have Jerry call me." "Sunday, 10:58 PM." "This is Louise Carter again. Jerry's still not home. Would one of you call me please?" "Monday, 10:22 AM." "Hey, Stan? Mr. Gilmore says if you don't show up or call today, you're fired. What's goin' on? Gimme a call." "Monday, 11:16 AM." "Hummmmmmmmmmmmmmmm (click)" "Monday, 4:05 PM." "Kenny, this is Danny. You were going to call me. This is important, and you know it. Call me right away." "Monday, 7:33 PM." "Mr. Stanley? This is Sheila Hitchcock with the Republican Party. As you know, making our country safe is a long, hard job. If the election were held today, who would you trust to lead our great nation in our time of need? Mr. Stanley?" "Tuesday, 6:22 PM." "Kenny! Pick up the fucking phone! Don't do this to me. Kenny, please. Don't be an asshole. Please, call me. Please." "Tuesday, 11:39 PM. End of messages."

Carter looked at me. "What's it all mean?"

"It means that whatever happened to your friend happened before he got to work on Saturday, and no one's heard from him. Where does he work?"

"Fabulous Footwear. It's in the Midtown Mall. Stan's the manager. Gilmore's the owner. What happened to Stan?"

"That's what we have to find out. 'Danny?' Is that his sister on the phone?"

"It could be. I haven't heard her voice in years, but she's the only one who'd call him Kenny. I didn't know she was back. Stan never said anything. Do you think Louise sounded worried?"

"When I met her, she didn't seem happy about getting a divorce. She said she still loved you. If that was Stanley's sister, we don't know that she's back. Just that they were in contact. Those could be long-distance calls. Where does Stanley keep his list of phone numbers?"

Like Carter, Stanley kept the top of his desk cleared. The only items on it were the phone, the message machine, and the same photo of Carter and Stanley with their string of fish. Carter opened the top right drawer and took out a Rolodex. The first card in the D's was new. It read "Danny—P 'n B" with a number but no area code. I dialed the number; a recorded voice said I had to first enter the area code. I redialed trying the local code.

A woman answered, but it wasn't Danny. "Puss 'n Boots."

I could hear country music in the background. It was similar to the noise in the background of Danny's messages.

"Hi. I'm trying to reach Danny Stanley. Is she there?"

"Don't know any Stanleys, but we got a Danny Steele that works here."

"That's probably her. Is she there?"

"No. She doesn't come on till six. Want to leave a message?"

"No, thank you. I'll stop by later. Good-bye."

I put the phone down. "Apparently Danny is working at a country bar. Is there a phone book?"

Carter took one out of the bottom drawer. "Do you think she knows anything?"

"Hard to say. She may or may not. Does Stanley have a will? Are there any other relatives?"

"I don't know. There wasn't anyone else when Stan inherited. You don't think Danny is behind this, do you?"

"Don't know and won't guess. Either way, I need to talk to her."

I looked up the address for Puss 'n Boots. It was located downtown on lower Clark Street, an older entertainment area of dubious reputation. A few years back, I'd cross the river occasionally and hit some bars along there but never heard of Puss 'n Boots. This was Captain Rod Rodecker's territory and I wasn't looking forward to being caught on his turf. Rod was an old friend from Army days, but my last trip over here put him and two of his detectives in a real jam.

"Is this house in the county or within the city limits?"

"Stan talked about annexation, but I think it's still county. Is it important?"

"No." Just another jurisdiction I'd like to avoid. "Stanley has a degree in political science. Why he is selling shoes?"

"No ambition. He inherited this place and sold off some of the land. He's not rich, but he's not hurting. How did you know about his degree?"

"I'm a detective. I couldn't get a credit report on him. Doesn't he use credit cards?"

"Doesn't believe in them. Pays cash for everything. What little he buys. Does it matter?"

"Credit cards and where they're used can be traced. It would help find him, or whoever was using the cards. What kind of car does he drive?"

"An old TR-6. British racing green. He's had it for years. I don't know the license number."

"I can get it. Okay, what was the Saturday routine?"

Carter took a deep breath. He seemed to be debating how much to tell me. Maybe he forgot how candid he'd been already.

"Usually Stan only works two Saturdays a month, but August is 'Back to School' specials, so he's there every weekend. He was supposed to get there at eight-thirty and get the place ready to open at nine. He woke me at six-thirty. I spent the night in the garage like you found me. It was part of my penance. He filled the dog bowls and helped me use the camp toilet. He came back when he was ready to leave. Said it was seven and that he'd be home by six. He usually has breakfast at the IHOP at the mall. When he would come home in the evening, my punishment would be over and we'd have the rest of the weekend together. That's the way it was supposed to happen."

"Okay. Show me around. Let's see if anything is out of place or missing."

Everything was neat and tidy and where it should be. The master bedroom was a second-story loft that looked down on the living room and out the wall of windows. The meadow and forest fell away from the house, and the river could be seen far away as a ribbon of light on the horizon.

A den was being used as a TV room. Stanley may not be rich, but he had a 54-inch LCD television on the wall. There were DVD and VHS video player/recorders and a sound system. There was a large collection of videos and a smaller one of DVDs. Westerns and war films predominated. He had what appeared to be a complete set of John Wayne films and the entire James Bond series. There were several porno videos, mostly gay oriented by their titles, and two untitled cassettes. There was a video camera on a tripod in the corner.

"Do you and Stanley record your activities?"

"Sometimes. Usually we just re-record over the same

tape."

"Sooner or later, if I don't find Stanley right away, the police will probably have to become involved. You might not want them finding films of you. On second thought, leave them. And don't clean up the garage. If anything's happened to Stanley, this is your alibi. It may be embarrassing, but it'll keep you from being a suspect. Did Stanley fool around with anyone else that you know about?"

"When he moved back here, he started going to places in town. I know he's had other relationships, but I don't know what he does when I'm not here. There is one place, a rough spot called the Manhole. Stan took me there once for punishment. People seemed to know him. We took a booth in the back. It's somewhere on lower Clark Street."

Great. Another place I don't want to go to.

"I'll check it out."

"You probably won't be welcome there."

"Tell me something I don't know."

I changed back into my own clothes after they dried. They were lightly wrinkled but suitable. When I thought Carter was able to drive, I sent him home. I said I'd call him when I found out anything. He left me his keys to the house.

As he drove away, I turned toward the garage. It was beyond my understanding how someone would seek out that kind of degradation, pain and suffering. When Archer and Tierney tortured me I was ready to accept death to escape them. When I felt my gun buried in the twisted bedclothes I was ready to kill to stop them. That Carter accepted — possibly found pleasure — in that kind of treatment mystified me. How different his first sexual experiences had been from mine. His had been controlled by a twisted sadistic personality. Mine . . . a tingly warmth flowed through me as I remembered Betty Jean Cooper.

"God, it's getting hot. Don't you think?"
I looked up from my bobber that was floating in the creek and

over to Betty Jean. She had on a beat-up straw hat over her dark, shoulder-length hair. She wore cut-off jeans and her short-sleeved, pink and green checked blouse was half unbuttoned and tied at the bottom. I wished again that I had small breasts like hers.

"Well, don't you?" she said again. "Even the fish aren't biting it's so hot."

"I guess we could hike back to my house. There's cold lemonade and I think some blackberry pie left over. Maybe some ice cream, too."

"That's a long, hot walk this time of day. At least it's shady here."

I looked up at the towering cottonwoods that shaded the bank and the deep hole in the creek we were fishing. The leaves were still – no breeze stirred them in the early summer heat.

"I know," Betty Jean said. "Let's go swimming."

"We didn't bring suits."

"Who needs them?"

She slowly blinked her doe-like eyes at me.

"I guess our clothes would dry on the walk home."

She blinked several times again. Did she have something in her eyes? She gave me her Mona Lisa smile.

"We could skinny-dip."

"Betty Jean! What if someone sees us?"

"Who's coming out here in this heat? Come on. It'll be fun. Chicken?"

We reeled in our lines. As I unbuttoned my blouse, Betty Jean already had hers off and was slipping off her pants. I turned away. I felt the heat of blush in my cheeks. This is silly, I thought. I'd seen Betty Jean naked before – in the school gym shower or at one of our houses when we stayed over together – but, somehow, out here on the bank of the creek, it was different. I heard her splash into the water. I hurriedly finished undressing and jumped in before I could change my mind.

The cool water took my breath away and I tingled all over from the sudden chill. We swam and splashed and floated the hot afternoon away. Then I felt Betty Jean's hand on my back. I turned, and she was right there – her face only inches away, her big brown *eyes so close, her arms folding around me, her lips coming to mine.*

I sighed at the memory, at that long ago age of innocence and went back into the house to make another search. I wore gloves, as I hadn't touched that much the first time through, and I didn't want to leave mixed messages for the police when they searched. I knew they would be searching. Stanley had been missing four days.

There wasn't much of interest to find. I pocketed a recent photo of Stanley and one of his sister when she was 17. She had pretty dark eyes, heavy brows and long dark hair in a ponytail. She wore a sport jersey and held a soccer ball. She'd be 30 now. I copied some names and numbers from the Rolodex but had no idea if I was missing someone important. Then I turned my attention to the home videos.

I didn't want to look at them. From the scene in the garage, I could guess what was on them. I was afraid of triggering another flashback. Until I found Carter, I hadn't had a really bad one in several weeks. But, to do my job right, I had to look. There was no cassette in the camera, but there was one already in the video player. It was of Carter and Stanley. Fortunately, there was nothing upsetting. Unfortunately, there was nothing to clue me into what happened to Stanley.

The two untitled cassettes on the shelves weren't blank. They were of Stanley and other people. Sometimes couples, sometimes groups, mostly men, but there were a few women. Some of it was nasty stuff, but most was pretty pedestrian for porn. The sound quality was poor and I heard no names. I fast-forwarded through most of it, stopping only to get a good look at faces that I might see in the next days. There was one face I had already seen, the clerk at the convenience store. It wasn't pepperoni he was feeding Stanley. I put things back as I found them.

I locked up, left several days' food and water for Amber, and headed back to the convenience store. The clerk was gone.

His name was Gordon. He'd be back in the morning. I knew he worked for Pizza Quick at night. I'd try to find him later. I drove into town.

Seven

THE IHOP AT THE Midtown Mall was near Main Street beside a Ruby Tuesday and an Arbys. Parking flowed into the mall lot. I spotted Stanley's green sports car. It was parked between the restaurants and the mall entrance. It was unlocked. The registration verified it as his. The keys were gone. Nothing seemed wrong. It was as neat and clean as his house. I went into IHOP.

I had the "Rooty Tooty, Fresh and Fruity" special and asked if there were anyone working that had been on the early shift Saturday morning. There wasn't. My waitress recognized the picture of Stanley. He came in once or twice a week for lunch or for coffee late in the afternoon. She hadn't seen him in a week. She didn't recognize Danny. I walked over to the mall.

Fabulous Footwear was a discount store: 40 to 60 percent off retail for last year's fashions. There were several women looking and trying on shoes, one clerk was helping a customer, and another was restocking shelves. I recognized the man at the register from one of the videotapes. He was early twenties with short curly blond hair. He had a pouty mouth and long-lashed blue eyes. The nametag on his white dress shirt identified him as Cameron and said he was the assistant manager.

"May I help you?" he asked my bosom.

I waited until he looked at my face. "Yes. I'm trying to find Kenneth Stanley. Have you seen him?"

"He doesn't work here anymore. Will there be anything else?"

I stood there looking at him and waited some more.

"What?" He blushed.

"You look different than on the videotape."

I gave him a flash of my State Association of Private Investigators membership card. It didn't have any authority, but it looked official.

"Maybe it's the clothes. Or lack thereof."

Color drained from his face. He looked around.

"Please, I can't talk here. Can we meet later?"

He hadn't asked, "What videotape?" I kept looking at him. He chewed his lip.

"Tom? I have to leave for a few minutes. Watch the register."

We sat on a bench in a quiet area of the mall. He kept looking around to see if anyone were watching.

"You really saw a videotape of me?"

I nodded. Staying quiet and staring often gets more information than asking questions.

"God forgive me. I thought someone was taking pictures, but I didn't really remember. I was kind of drunk. I never did anything like that before. I swear. Oh, God. I'm not like that. There was this party, you see. Lots of wine and some pot. I got too drunk, or something. Jesus, help me. It seemed so natural at the time. Everyone was into it. You know what I mean? I couldn't help myself. Stan asked me back a couple of times, but I didn't go. With God's blessings, I resisted temptation."

When he paused, I didn't say anything, just continued to stare. Gave him no help.

"It wasn't my kind of scene, you know? You have to understand. That was okay with Stan; he didn't press or anything, but I always wondered if there were pictures. That was months ago. You have to understand; I'm married now. I don't know what people will think if they ever find out; if my wife found out. Can I get the tape?"

"I don't think so. The police may need to see it. Where's Stanley?"

"The police?" He turned pale.

"Where's Stanley?"

"I don't know. Honest. He didn't open up Saturday. That's never happened before. I called, but he didn't answer. I thought maybe he had one of his parties and overslept. I had to call Mr. Gilmore to come in with the keys. When Stan didn't come in on Monday, Gilmore fired him and made me assistant manager. Gilmore was very angry. He had the locks changed. You can really recognize me on the tape?"

"Lots of face. Lots of action."

"Oh, God. Why would the police need to see it?"

"Stanley's missing. If he doesn't show up damn soon, the police will investigate just like I'm doing. They'll ask questions, and, after they see the tape, they'll come back and ask more questions."

Cameron buried his face in his hands. "God? What am I going to do? What should I do?"

"Tell the truth. When did you last see Stanley?"

He sat there shaking his head, looking at the ground, thinking or praying. Then he looked up.

"Friday night. He locked up at nine. Said he'd see me in the morning."

"When did you get here Saturday?"

"Ten till nine. When he wasn't here, I called to see if he was running late. I waited to call Mr. Gilmore until ten after. I was hoping Stan would show up."

"Did Stanley say anything else Friday night? Ask you to another party, for instance?"

"No. We just talked about the 'Back to School' sale. He stopped asking me to parties quite a while ago."

"And you haven't seen or heard from him since Friday?"

"No."

"You said Gilmore fired him Monday. Did Gilmore speak to him?"

"No. We couldn't reach him. Gilmore sent him a letter."

Was Gilmore's letter among the stuff in the mailbox?

"One more thing. Did you know anyone else at the party?"

"No. I'd never seen them before or since."

"Can you remember any names?"

He thought about it and shook his head.

"Sorry. It was six, eight months ago. I've tried to forget it. I've prayed constantly for God's forgiveness."

"Okay. Thanks. If you remember anything more about the party or anything else—like maybe a customer that Stanley was talking to too closely—give me a call. It could be important." I gave him my card.

STANLEY DISAPPEARED BETWEEN seven and nearly nine Saturday morning. His car was in the parking lot. Did he disappear before or after breakfast? Who could have seen him? Maybe I'd find out in the morning.

It was early and the night crowds hadn't arrived when I pulled onto lower Clark Street. There was plenty of parking available along the curb. I found Puss 'n Boots. Its animated sign was a dancing cat in a cowboy hat and boots.

The place was large and low lit: booths and tables, long bar, a large dance area with a stage for a band. Drums were already set up. A single couple swayed on the dance floor as some guy lamented from the jukebox about a lost saltshaker. There were about a dozen people in all, including the waitress and bartender. Most were dressed western style with high-crowned cowboy hats. All were women. Most were staring at me.

Were my leading elements causing the disturbance as usual? Or was it my wrinkled jacket, slacks and pumps? I didn't fit the local décor. I went to the bar. The bartender, a six-footer with super-short hair cut in what could be called a 'fade' and dyed an unnatural yellow with red streaks, came over. She had heavy dark Brooke Shields' eyebrows and was deeply tanned for someone who worked indoors. She filled out her blue Western shirt with white piping nicely: meaning a size I wished to be. The mother-of-pearl buttons on the pockets were right where her nipples would be.

"Welcome, darlin'. Are you lost or slummin'?"

"I'm looking for someone."

"Aren't we all? You a cop or a process server?"

"Why not just a customer meeting a date?"

"You're not dressed for it. Not here anyway."

Her smile was nice; I felt my lips curling in reply. She had high cheekbones and dark bedroom eyes.

"So which is it?"

"Private cop. But I'm not serving paper. Just looking for information. Is Danny Steele here? I understand she works here."

The bartender's eyes narrowed and her smile dimmed. "We sell drinks, not info. What are you drinkin'?"

"Any single malt Scotch?"

"Probably one of the Glens, right? Not here. I got some Johnnie Walker and J&B, but that's it. We're more Jack and margaritas." Her smile was back. "Especially margaritas. Hell, half the twat in here are Parrotheads. How 'bout I just bring you a draft?"

I didn't understand the "Parrothead" reference, so while she got my drink, I looked around. There were a couple carved wooden parrots behind the bar and one hanging on a perch from the ceiling. In one corner were fake palm trees and three women were wearing Hawaiian shirts. I still hadn't a clue. The dancers had retreated to a booth and were sharing a large margarita. The waitress had disappeared. I hadn't gotten a good look at her and wondered if she were Danny. I put a twenty on the bar.

The bartender put down my beer, scooped up the twenty, went to the register and returned with three singles, three fives and a bucket of peanuts.

"Not very busy tonight," I said, trying to be friendly.

"It's early. We got line dance lessons at eight. There's a buffet startin' at nine and dancin' till the cows come home after that. Stick around. It's a nice crowd."

Her smile was engaging and the invitation tempting. I wouldn't mind waltzing her around the floor a few times with some horizontal tango later.

Damn. I've got a hot lover at home and I'm contemplating a one-night stand? What's got into me? You're horny and can't get enough, that's what. Control yourself. Breathe deep.

I pushed the change to the bartender. "About Danny. Is she here?"

She pushed the money back. "What do you want with her?"

Protective? Is this a big sister or something?

"It has to do with her brother."

"Kenny? What's happened to Kenny?"

She dropped the thick, country drawl. Now I recognized the voice from the phone. She didn't look anything like her photo. I hadn't realized how tall she was. In the photo of Carter and Stanley, Stanley was a lot taller; Carter was about five-ten. It looked like tallness was a Stanley family trait. The face was similar to Stanley's also: long with high cheekbones. The hair fooled me. Shit. I was thinking about hitting on a possible suspect, the twisted sister herself. Not good. Not good at all.

"He's missing. Have you seen him? Do you know where he is?"

"What do you mean 'missing?' How did you find me, anyway?"

"Hey, Danny," the waitress called from down the bar. "I need four margaritas and a pair of longnecks."

I watched Danny make the drinks and make change for the waitress. She still looked good to me—What about Wendy?—but I remembered what Carter had told me about his and Stanley's sexual introduction. What was Danny into these days? The same singer as before was playing again on the jukebox. He still hadn't found that saltshaker.

"You said Kenny's missing. When?"

How much to tell her? How much does she know?

"Since Saturday morning. Never showed up for work. Isn't at his house. I was hired today to find him. You left messages on his machine. Have you seen him or heard from him?"

"No, not a word. He was supposed to call me over the weekend, but never did. What happened to him?"

"Don't know yet. He's not in a hospital as far as I know. Why was he calling you?"

"Danny? Two drafts and two shots of Jack."

She went to fill the order. Before she came back, two string beans came in and sat at the bar. They were wiry and had been poured into their new jeans that were pulled over their hand-tooled boots. Their Western shirts were fitted and crisp, their itty-bitty breasts barely making dents in the fabric. They wore high-crowned Stetsons pulled low over the eyes. I heard one murmur, "Check out the heifer in mufti." The other one whispered back, "I'd sure like to milk that."

I hate my breasts because they're heavy and a strain on the body, and often because of the undue attention they bring. When I can get enough saved up, I'll have them trimmed down, but as much as I hate them, I don't like people—women or men—making sexist comments. I felt like tossing my beer at them, but didn't want to make a scene. I needed information from Danny. She came back down the bar putting two bottles of Corona with limes in front of the string beans. They asked her something but all I heard was her saying, "cop."

"It's getting too busy to talk now, but I need to know

what's going on. We close at two. Can you stick around?"

"I'll come back. There are a couple more things I can check on."

I started to leave the money on the bar, but Danny took only one of the singles and pushed the rest to me.

Eight

I STOOD ACROSS THE STREET from the Manhole watching men go in and out. There was a lot of tight leather, chains and tattoos. Carter had said it was a rough place and that I wouldn't be welcome. I believed him. I saw the tapes and how Stanley treated Carter. This was a place Stanley frequented, therefore—

"Well, if it ain't the dickless wonder from the big city?"

Jabba the Hutt waddled toward me. Shit. So much for avoiding the cops.

"Hi, Jabba. Still the useless dick, I see."

"It's Detective Jablowski, and I'm dick enough to pull your tits out of the wringer."

True enough. Jabba and his partner had jumped jurisdiction and helped rescue me. I didn't know it at the time—which is no excuse—but I had never thanked him. Jabba and I don't exactly get along.

"Look, Jabba, I really appreciate what you guys did for me."

"Yeah, right. No big deal. We just shoved your ass into Taylor's car so he could rush you to the hospital; though he didn't tell us the hospital was outta state. Then we stood around with our thumbs up our asses while Captain 'Hot

Rod' explains why we were interferin' at a county crime scene. That's all."

"Well, thanks anyway; and the flowers at the hospital were nice."

"Wasn't my idea."

"Really? Never would have guessed. I heard you got a commendation after they found the buried bodies. That must look good in your file, Jabba."

"Yeah. We skated, no thanks to you. And stop calling me 'Jabba.' My name's Jablowski. You got no memory, or what? Speaking of bad memory, why are you back over here, anyway?"

"Hey, Wayne. It didn't pan out. Bird doesn't know the guy." Detective Carson walked up. "We're going to have to keep . . . Oh. Hi, Miss Cord. What are you doing here?"

"That's what I'm asking her."

"Please, call me Rachel."

I shook Detective Carson's hand. I knew he had had a crush on me. Did he ever find out I was a lesbian?

"I just wanted to thank the two of you for helping me."

"I'm Mike. This is Wayne. You came all the way down here to thank us?"

Jabba cut in. "I think she's working without a license again. Let's run her in."

"Wayne? Is that your middle name, by any chance?"

"What's it to ya?"

"Just curious. Well, thanks again. Both of you. I can see you're busy. Maybe we can get together some time over a drink." I looked at Jabba's gut. "Or a case of doughnuts."

I turned to walk away.

"Wait a minute."

Shit. I had to say "doughnuts." When will I ever . . . I turned back. They weren't smiling.

"Why are you here?" Carson asked.

"Looking for a friend."

"You don't have any," Jabba chimed in. "Where does this

'friend' live?"

"In the country, but I thought he might be in town."

"Jesus, Mary and Joseph." Jabba looked to the sky. "Here we go again. Let's run her in."

"Which will it be, Rachel?" Carson asked. "Tell us here or tell it to Rodecker in the morning, *after* a night in holding."

I knew they weren't kidding. I showed them Stanley's picture and gave them the condensed version about his being missing and worried family and friends. I didn't tell them about finding Carter and didn't say I was being paid.

"There's no law against asking questions."

Jabba put his finger in my face. "There is here if you're working as a dick and got no license."

"Why haven't these family and friends reported it?" Carson asked.

"No one knew he was missing until today. If I didn't find out anything by tomorrow, I was going to recommend calling the police."

"Sure you were," Jabba sneered.

Carson looked up and down the street and across to the Manhole.

"The guy's into kinky sex, and you think he might be in there; or someone there might know where he is. Is that it?"

"Mike. You're not thinking of helping this bitch, are you? We coulda lost our pensions for cryin' out loud."

Carson ignored Jabba and kept looking at me.

"Detective Jablowski's right, Mike. You got in big trouble for helping me last time. Thank you. I'll tell my . . . friends that they need to call the police."

"Wayne, this won't take long; we'd just have to come back and ask the same questions again once it's reported."

Jabba shook his head. "No, we won't. Because someone else will get the case, not us."

"Who else gets stuck with cases down here? You know it'll come to us."

Jabba looked to the sky again; he was waffling. "Gimme

one reason we should care about this twink that likes it kinky?"

Carson sighed. "Because he's a fellow human being."

I kept my mouth shut. I didn't want them remembering it would probably be a Sheriff's investigation, considering Stanley's address. Then again, he had disappeared here in town.

After more arguing, they led me across the street. We entered the Manhole.

Restrooms were at the front. They were marked "MEN" and "REAL MEN." The room was long, narrow and dark. A bar ran along one side with stools; deep booths ran along the other. At the end of the room was a safety barrier around an open manhole with a sign reading "MEN WORKING." Music echoed up through the hole.

A behemoth rose from the first stool. He was over seven-foot and as wide as a side-by-side refrigerator. He wore a black leather vest with no shirt and tight leather pants. Tattoos covered his bald head, arms, chest and probably everything else. He stared down at me through round blue-lensed glasses.

"No women allowed."

He would have been more intimidating if he didn't sound like Tweety Bird. His eyes widened and he backed off. I looked over my shoulder. Both Carson and Jabba had their shields out for Big Bird to see. One of the bartenders came to our end of the room.

"It's okay, Tiny. I got it." He raised his voice. "Evening, officers. Is anything wrong?"

There was sudden activity in some of the booths along the wall. I couldn't see what it was, but I could hear it. One or two faces appeared to see what was happening, then disappeared again.

Carson took the lead. "We're looking for someone. Have you seen this man?"

I showed him the picture of Stanley.

"Not tonight. He comes in occasionally, two, three times a month."

"When did you see him last?"

"A week or so ago. What's he done?"

"You haven't seen him since Saturday?"

"No. It's been at least a week."

"Who does he hang with?"

"No one in particular. He's usually cruising when he comes here."

"Mind if we look around and ask your customers?

"Help yourselves. You're the Man." He went back behind the bar.

The room was quiet. The music below had stopped. Jabba pushed past moving more quickly than I thought he could to the emergency exit and went out. We heard his voice.

"All right, ladies. Back in the Hole."

Everyone at the bar and in the booths was sitting upright with his hands in sight. Good little choirboys all dressed in leather, ready for their Sunday lesson. We worked the room methodically but quickly, showing the picture, asking the same questions. "Do you know this man?" "When did you last see him?" "Did you go out with him?" "Where might we find him?" "Who might know him?"

We got no help. I didn't see anyone I recognized from the videos. When we reached the end of the room, I saw Jabba outside, standing at the top of a flight of stairs in the alley. He spoke to Carson.

"Half a dozen got away. The rest are waiting for you."

Carson and I climbed down the manhole. The room below was three times larger than the one above and the lighting wasn't any better. It was all booths around three walls, a dance floor and bandstand. Four musicians sat at the edge of the bandstand. Half the booths were filled. Jabba stood in the open exit door.

Carson moved to the middle of the dance floor. He showed his shield.

"We're going to ask everyone some simple questions; then we'll leave. No hassles. No problems."

We started in the restrooms to see if anyone were hiding. In one stall, a man was sitting with his pants around his ankles. He didn't like being disturbed in his private business, but he answered the questions. In another stall we found a man in a nice business suit crouching on top of a toilet so his feet wouldn't show.

"I haven't done anything," he said before we could even ask. "I've never been here before. Honest." He was no help either.

We made the rounds of the booths and came up with negative answers. When we were done, I led Carson and Jabba back to one booth.

"These two. They're lying. I saw them on a tape with Stanley."

"Why don't you come with us outside and explain why you lied."

They denied they were lying, but Carson was insistent. Jabba pulled one up. The other followed. We went out the emergency exit to the alley.

"I don't like being lied to," Jabba said to the one he was holding. "Let's go have a private talk." He hauled the guy down the alley.

"Where are they going?" the other guy asked.

Carson moved him to the wall. "For a private talk. Maybe we just don't want you guys trading stories. Maybe my partner doesn't want you seeing how he asks questions when he's lied to. Alleys are dangerous places. You never know what you might trip over or fall into. A person could get hurt."

There was the sound of a trash can being knocked over. The guy looked down the alley then back at Carson.

"This is the way it's going to be. I'm going to ask some questions; you're going to tell me the truth. If you lie, I may think you're hiding something and have to search you. Who knows what I may find? Hell. You might have a weapon, and I'd have to shoot you to protect myself. Or, I may think you're an accomplice to the guy we're looking for and have to arrest you. So let's not waste your time or mine. Okay? Rachel?"

"Yes?"

"Go to the end of the alley and keep a lookout."

"Why? I can see if anyone comes in from here. I want to hear what this guy has to say."

"Two reasons. One, you're not a police officer and don't belong here. Two, I don't want a witness to my interrogation technique. Now go."

I didn't like it, but I did as he said and waited at the end of the alley. I paced back and forth and kept looking back. Even with lights over emergency exits, there were too many shadows. I couldn't see anything. I almost wished I smoked, just for something to do. Twenty minutes later, Carson and Jabba came laughing down the alley. The two guys were gone.

"What did you do to them? What did they say?"

"We didn't do anything," Jabba said, "except let their imaginations run away with them."

"They said they partied with your friend a few times. Sometimes at his place, sometimes other places. They hadn't seen him in a couple of weeks. He likes it rough, and he likes to take pictures."

"Any leads?"

"A couple names. A couple addresses."

"There was one guy," Jabba said. "No name. Your friend brought him in about six months ago on a leash. Made him sit under the table and give blowjobs to anyone that sat down. Maybe he's behind your friend's disappearance. Payback. Know what I mean?" Jabba shook his head. "You got strange friends."

The guy on the leash was probably Carter. He had said that Stanley brought him here for punishment. I needed those names and addresses.

"What are the names? The addresses?"

"That's for us to check out," Carson said, putting up his hand to stop my complaint. "When we get an official request, that is. No more favors. Call your clients—excuse me— 'friends and family.' Tell them to call us and report the guy missing. It's been more than four days; it doesn't look good. I'll check the morgue, just in case. Now, go home. Wayne and I have work to do."

Nine

IF CARSON AND JABBA thought they could run me off that easily, they were sorely mistaken. I was pissed. I really wanted that information, but had no way of getting it now. It was after nine; maybe I could find my clerk.

I drove back to Stanley's place and rechecked the mailbox. Nothing new had been added. There were a couple bills, a magazine and the letter from the shoe store. I took them to the house.

Amber was curled up on one of the wicker chairs. She got down, rubbed against me, and followed me in. I put my gloves back on and found the number to Pizza Quick. They asked for the phone number. I gave it and said I wanted the usual order.

I turned on the TV and VCR; found the tape I wanted, cued it, put the remote control in my pocket and took a copy of *Time* from the magazine rack. Then Amber and I went back to the porch to wait for the delivery boy. I turned my cell phone on and called Wendy.

"Hi. Are you at home?"

"No. I'm still across the river. It looks like I may be here all night."

"Too bad. I was hoping to come over and we could order

out."

"That would have been nice. Sorry. I have a couple of leads I still need to follow tonight. Then another one early in the morning. Maybe tomorrow night?"

"I'd like that. You haven't found the husband yet?"

"Found him and found a bigger mess. He's hired me to find someone else. That's what I'm doing now. It's too complicated to explain over the phone. I'll tell it to you tomorrow."

"Okay. I have some information for you on re-financing your mortgage, and . . . and there's another idea I'd like you to consider. We can talk about that tomorrow night too. I miss you."

"I miss you too. Goodnight."

Complicated. Got that right. Especially when I'm attracted to a possibly wacko bartender when I already have wonderful Wendy. Should have my head examined. Wonder if Dr. Howard would do a telephone consult this late. I checked my voicemail for messages. There were three from Frank Taylor, my police friend who had "rushed me back across the river" as Jabba had said.

The first one was from this morning. I really should check messages more often.

"Rachel, this is Frank. Call me. I've left messages at your office. Don't you work anymore?"

Ouch. That hurt. The second one was mid-afternoon.

"Rachel, Frank again. Don't you ever have your phone on? We need to talk."

What was going on? The last one was at six this evening.

"Girl, you better not be avoiding me. This is serious. Do I have to put out an APB to find you?"

Girl? That didn't sound like Frank. He never calls me *girl.* He's never condescending. My personal "Papa Bear," a friend and father figure for several years. I spent Fourth of July with him and his family. We have lunch regularly. How did I piss him off?

I hadn't been in the office since Monday, so had no idea what messages Frank left there. I don't like being called on my cell. It can interfere with what I'm doing, so I tend to keep it off unless I'm expecting a call. I hadn't checked messages. Bad habit, but that's . . . maybe I should call him. But he might want to see me right away. Tonight even. Too much to do; it'll have to wait until I get home. I turned the phone off in case Frank tried calling again.

Lights were coming up the drive. My pizza was here.

As I had hoped, Gordon was the delivery boy. I picked up the copy of *Time* and opened the porch door. Halfway to the porch he stopped. He looked surprised.

"Hey. Didn't expect to see you again. Did you find Mr. Carter?"

"Yes, thank you. Now I'm house-sitting. Come on in. My money's in the den."

"Where's Mr. Stanley?"

"He's away."

I led him through the house. The smell of pepperoni made my mouth water. As I walked I rolled the magazine into a tight cylinder. It might not look like it, but a rolled up magazine makes a formidable weapon. Magazine paper is mostly wood pulp. Rolled tightly it's like a 12-inch piece of broom handle. It'll do a lot of damage. I didn't know if I really needed it, but I like to play safe.

"Put the pizza on the coffee table, please. How much do I owe you?"

"$14.68 with tax."

Gordon was facing the TV as he put the pizza down. I pressed PLAY on the VCR remote. The sound and picture startled him. I let the tape run for several seconds. Two men were having sex: Gordon and Stanley. I pressed PAUSE. Gordon turned. I held the rolled magazine low to my side.

"I can explain. It's not what you think. Really."

"It's exactly what I think. Sit down."

He tried to get past me. I brought the magazine up

quickly, jamming it into his abdomen. He retched; grabbed me to hold himself up. I helped him into a chair. I waited until he got his breath back and some of the redness left his face. Beads of sweat had popped out on his brow.

I pulled up his shirt to check damage. There was a red mark about an inch across between his sternum and navel. The skin wasn't broken. I touched it. He winced and breathed in sharply. He'd have a bruise, but I didn't think there was serious damage. You have to be careful. Too hard a blow like that could rupture internal organs. It could kill.

"Why did you do that?"

"Tell me about you and Stanley."

"There's nothing to tell. He buys gas and stuff at the store. I deliver pizza to him at night."

I pressed PLAY again.

"Turn it off. Please."

Gordon turned his face away putting a hand to his eyes. I waited a few moments.

"Were you expecting to find Stanley here?"

He nodded. "It was his order. Last delivery of the night."

"Is that how it usually went?"

He nodded again. "I'd pay for the pizza and turn in all my receipts so I wouldn't have to go back to the shop. Then I'd come here."

"How long's it been going on?"

"Two years. Since the third or fourth time I delivered out here."

"How old are you?"

He hesitated. "Nineteen."

"You were *seventeen* when this started?"

"Almost eighteen. Stan didn't know it. I lied about my age so I could work at the store and drive for Pizza Quick. Everyone thinks I'm twenty."

"So you, Stanley, Carter, and the others—"

"Not Mr. Carter. Never Mr. Carter. They always ordered their pizza early on Saturday nights. I don't think Mr. Carter knew about me, or the others."

"When did you last see Stanley?"

"Thursday night. I brought a pizza and spent the night."

"Anyone else here?"

"No, just the two of us. If there was a party, he'd order more pizza."

"Did he ever take you anywhere else?"

"No."

"The others you met here, have you seen or been with any of them anywhere else?"

He hesitated again. "No."

"Why the hesitation? Who is it?"

"I don't want to get anyone in trouble. Where's Stan?"

"He's missing. I don't care about the sex. I'm looking for leads to find him. He may be hurt. He may need help. You can help. Who is it?"

"A couple. Jackie and Dorian. I don't know their last name. I've been to their house."

Gordon gave me the address and directions. They lived on my side of the river. At least I could check them out without getting into trouble. We scanned the videos to see if they were in them. There were clear shots of Jackie — she liked the camera — but not Dorian, only his back.

I sent Gordon home with the change from the bar and an extra twenty. I found a blank cassette and made a copy of the portions of the sex tape with Jackie and Dorian. I put that in my bag. I put the tapes back the way I had found them.

I shared a couple slices of pizza with Amber after removing the hot peppers. Neither of us cared for those.

"So, Amber. Any idea where Stanley is?"

The cat tilted its head and mouthed silently. She may have been asking, "What, no anchovies?", then went back to eating the pepperoni and cheese.

Stanley liked his sex rough and kinky. Did that have anything to do with his disappearance? Why, when he had a weekend planned with Carter? Why was his car still at the mall? I had more paths to follow, but no clear idea of where they would lead. I had to talk with Danny. What was her involvement?

I found an ironing board and iron and took the wrinkles out of my slacks and jacket.

Trying to impress Danny?

No, just being neat.

Liar.

Shut up.

IT WAS NEARLY MIDNIGHT when I got back to Puss 'n Boots. The dance floor was full. Everyone moved in lines doing some kind of choreographed step to the music of a four-piece women's band. The buffet to the side was pretty well picked over. There were a few chicken wings and carrots left, but that was about it. Good thing I had the pizza. I made my way to the bar.

There were two bartenders working. Danny saw me, came over and set a beer in front of me. She told me to follow her. At the end of the bar, she took a fringed buckskin jacket from a hook on the wall.

"Put this on," she said in my ear over the noise.

I took off my jacket, putting my keys, ID and cash into my slacks pockets. My cell phone was in my bag in the trunk of the car. Danny helped me on with the buckskin. She smoothed it across my shoulders and down my arms. The jacket was tight across my bosom so I left it open. I turned around.

She leaned in close. "Now you won't stick out *quite* so much."

There was laughter in her voice. Her cheek brushed mine. I felt a blush coming and took a deep breath. She pulled a bolo tie with a silver and turquoise slide from her pocket and put it over my head. She adjusted it for me. Gee, mama, am I all dressed now?

"We can talk later."

I sat at the bar, sipping my beer and watching the dancers. The moves looked complicated, but everyone was right in step. Those not dancing were clapping along and shouting encouragement. I'm not a big country fan, but the music was infectious. Danny came over, leaned across the bar and yelled above the din.

"Do you drink tequila?"

I shook my head. She left and came back with two shots of Jack Daniel's.

"These are from Mollie and Cassie." She pointed down the bar.

The two string beans were back and looking my way. One tipped her hat to me, and the other raised a shot glass. I raised a glass back and took a sip. I watched her down the shot and bite into a lime. I guessed she liked tequila. They came over.

"May we join you?"

"As long as we get three things straight. One, I'm spoken for. Two, I'm not a heifer. Three, I don't need milking."

I downed the shot of Jack and slammed the glass on the bar. They blushed, looked away and then apologized.

"This is Mollie. I'm Cassie. Would you care to dance?"

Cassie as in Cassandra? What warnings do you have?

"I can't dance like that."

"Sure you can. Come on."

They each held an arm and led me to the dance floor. We joined a line in the back where my stumbles wouldn't be as easily noticed. Before the band started the next song, they gave me a quick dry run lesson. I felt foolish, but there were also others just learning, and the group laughter wasn't aimed at anyone. It was everyone having fun. As the song played, I couldn't hear the words over my own internal "one two three four five six seven and, one two three four . . ."

By 1:45, the crowd had thinned. The music changed back to the jukebox and that guy who couldn't find his saltshaker. The band was dancing with some of the customers. Cassie was moving about the floor with the lead singer. Mollie and I had our backs to the bar watching. At some point, I ended up wearing her hat. She had moved close enough so that our arms were touching, but she hadn't put any other moves on me yet.

I tried to remember how much I had had to drink. I bought a round, so there had been at least three shots of Jack. Two beers, or was the half one on the bar my third? Fourth? Were there more? I had made two trips to the restroom, so maybe, but I wasn't sure. I had eaten a couple of the leftover wings and some carrots, and a hunk of cheese and slice of rye I found. I wasn't at my best, and I still hadn't talked with Danny.

"You gals need a refill? This is last call."

"No more for me, thanks."

Mollie shook her head. "No thanks."

Danny went over and put some quarters in the jukebox. She came back and held out her hand to me. I took it. She reached up and removed the hat I was wearing and returned it to Mollie. I gave Mollie a kind of I-told-you-I-was-spoken-for tilt of my head. She nodded and gave a maybe-next-time smile.

Danny walked me to the dance floor. "Sorry. We won't be able to talk until after I close out."

"Not a problem."

She took me in her arms and led me about to the slow strains of the *Tennessee Waltz*. The song brought back pleasant, safe memories—it was my mother's favorite—of dancing about the living room in my prepubescent youth. Danny was a good dancer, totally in control. Her eyes never left mine. Her hand at the small of my back pressed or gave way perfectly, guiding me around the floor. The song played twice before we went back to the bar.

I didn't see Cassie. She and the lead singer had left. Mollie was waiting. Danny went behind the bar.

Mollie got off of her stool. "Time for me to head for the

barn. Thanks for the dances."

"It was fun. I enjoyed it. Thank you."

She took my hand, kissed it, then moved in close and gave me a long soulful kiss: something to remember her by; something to let me know what I was missing; maybe, something to look forward to. She winked and left.

I was still wearing Danny's buckskin when we left the bar. I carried my jacket over my arm. The cool, night air helped clear the fuzzies as I breathed it in. We walked to my car. The street was pretty deserted.

"It's only a few blocks, but do you want me to drive?"

"No, I can handle it."

I unlocked the doors then saw the police car waiting down the street. There were two silhouettes inside.

"On second thought, yes, you can drive."

As we passed the police car, I looked over to the two uniformed officers and smiled. I watched in the side mirror as their lights went on, they did a U-turn and followed. Danny made a couple of turns and pulled into an old motel right on the river with individual cabins. The sign read "Rustic on the River, daily and weekly rates, kitchenettes. NO VACANCY." There were 12 units. Danny parked in front of number 9.

I left my jacket in the car, but retrieved my bag from the trunk. The police car was parked at the street. We could hear the squawk of the radio.

"What do they want?"

I shrugged. "Checking for drunk drivers, probably." Or following unlicensed detectives. "Can we go down to the river? My head's still not clear."

"This way."

We went between the cabins and followed a path to a wooden staircase that went down to a small beach. There were two picnic tables and grills and three fire rings. The glow from my city across the river reflected on the water and obscured many of the stars. We gathered driftwood and built a fire; sat on cinder blocks and poked sticks into the flames.

Marshmallows would have been nice, with graham crackers and chocolate bars.

I heard a faint squawking and looked up the embankment. I could barely discern a silhouette from the background darkness. What was I doing here? Why didn't I just stay on my side of the river? Were Carson and Jabba having me watched? Or was it Frank? Did he put out that APB on me? What did he want that was so important?

"Rachel? What's happened to my brother?"

I refocused on the here and now. "I don't know yet. I'm trying to find him. He's been missing four days. Five now. Maybe he's all right, maybe he's not. When did you last see him?"

"Eleven, twelve years ago, I guess. Hard to remember. Do you remember what you were doing twelve years ago?"

"Guarding sand. I was an MP during the Gulf War stationed in Saudi and Kuwait. So you haven't seen him since you ran away? When did you come back?"

"About six weeks ago. Living here and working at P 'n B. How did you know I ran away?"

"Jerome Carter. You made a lasting impression on him and your brother. They're still involved with each other, and he hired me to find Stanley."

"Jerry? He's still around? And he and Kenny are . . . Wow. Wow, that blows my mind."

She stared into the fire, poked at the embers, stirred up a new blaze.

"Ah, did he tell you anything . . . anything about . . ."

"In graphic detail." I watched her squirm. She wouldn't look at me. "Why was your brother supposed to call you? What was so important?"

She didn't answer right away. I waited.

"When I came back, I didn't know my parents were dead. It took me three weeks to get up enough courage to call out there. The number was still the same. They hadn't seen or heard from me since I left. Kenny answered the phone. He told me about the car accident. He was bitter and cruel. Didn't want anything to do with me. I guess I deserved that.

"Their deaths shocked me. Whether anyone believes it or not, I loved my parents. I guess I always thought I could go home again. I called back a week later. We yelled at each other. I cried. We finally talked. I called back twice after that. We talked more. Laid some demons to rest, I think. Neither of us suggested getting together. The last time I called was a week ago. I asked Kenny if he still had Mom and Dad's personal things. Asked if I could have something, just something. I didn't have anything to remember them, and I wanted to . . . Kenny said he would think about it. Said he would call me over the weekend. He never called."

"You haven't seen him at all?"

"No."

I passed her the photo I had of him in my bag. She turned it into the light from the fire.

"Wow. Good lookin' guy. Looks like a store mannequin. Can you find him?" She passed the photo back.

"I'm trying, but someone needs to report his disappearance to the police. You're his sister. It should be you."

"Let me think about it."

The fire died down. We scattered the embers and walked up the stairs back to my car.

"Would you like to stay?"

Would I? No! Go home! Get a motel room! Stay at Stanley's! Any place but here!

I looked across the parking lot. The police car was still waiting.

Danny saw it too. "What do they still want?"

"Watching me, most likely. Some people don't like me asking questions on this side of the river."

"In that case, you better stay here. You had a lot to drink. If they pull you over now, you'll test above the limit, and they'll run you in."

"You're probably right."
No! No! No! No! Yes.

Ten

A JANGLING ALARM CLOCK startled me. An elbow dug into my side and the mattress was too soft. An arm reached across me. A bare breast dangled above me, the nipple brushing my nose. The jangling stopped. Danny flopped back onto the bed.

"God, it's too early. What time is it?"

I looked at the clock. "Seven."

My head was fuzzy from not enough sleep and too much drink. I got out of bed. The jangling started again — in my head this time — as I fumbled about searching the room. The drapes were closed, but light seeped through giving the room a warm shadowed glow. One of my shoes with my knee-highs stuffed in it was by the chair where my slacks hung neatly. The other shoe was near the door. Where was my blouse? On a hanger, at least, on the closet door. Shook my head to clear the cobwebs. Shouldn't have done that. My panties were buried under the covers at the end of the bed. Where in hell was my bra?

"Come back to bed."

"Can't. I need to interview someone early. Have you seen my —"

Danny brought up my bra from beside her side of the

bed.

"Thanks. Can I use your shower?"

"Why not? You used everything else."

Her leering laughter followed as I beat a hasty retreat. I leaned against the bathroom door, catching up with myself. My head hurt. I found aspirin above the sink and took three; drank two glasses of water. I looked awful. Drank another glass of water. There were dark shadows around my eyes like I had been hit. My eyes were bloodshot. There was a bottle of eye drops. I used it and got in the shower.

The water was slow getting hot and the cold woke me fully. I ached in many places. My nipples were raw and tender. Scratches stung my back. My left shoulder had been bit. My vulva bruised.

Sex with Danny was a very different world from that with Wendy. Where Wendy was a warm, flowing, melting into one another, Danny was a no holds barred give and take—and then some. I soothed my vulva remembering how it got that way.

Danny liked it hard and rough. At some point in our lust, she fitted me with a strap-on dildo. The bruising came from the strap-on as I pummeled her, jamming it again and again into her—all of her—until I was exhausted. As I did, visions of Archer and Tierney came back, and it was if I were pummeling them—wreaking vengeance for what they had done. It was wrong, way wrong, but I did it anyway.

I had been drunk and keyed up from yesterday's flashback, but that was no excuse. I wanted to blame Archer and Tierney, blame Danny in some way. But like the guy on the jukebox kept saying, it was my own damn fault. I felt shamed. I let the hot water blister me. Wanted it to purge me—drain me—of the guilt of my actions. Not that it did. And Wendy? What could I possibly tell Wendy?

Danny peeked at me from under a pillow as I came out of the bathroom drying my hair, another towel wrapped around me.

"Are you all right?"

"I think so. You?"

"Worn out. You're a real rough rider."

I dropped to the floor beside the bed.

"I'm sorry. I'm sorry. I shouldn't—"

"Hey. Hey, there. It's okay. I'm fine. Really. I got what I wanted. I'm a sick bitch, didn't you know?" She smiled. "Next time wear spurs."

She pulled my face to hers; kissed me long and hungrily; made me want to crawl in, take her again. I finally, reluctantly, pulled away.

"I've got to get going."

"I'd rather have you coming."

She laughed as I did a full body blush.

I pulled on yesterday's panties and found my bag. I sat at the small dresser, brushed my hair, fixed my make-up to lessen the shadows around my eyes. Danny watched as I harnessed my breasts. It's not an easy operation. I have to lean forward at the waist so my watermelons hang free and fit them into the bra cups and adjust the straps. It's a strain on the lower back. I'd rather have peaches, but I'll settle for grapefruit someday.

"Rachel?"

"Yes?"

"I can't afford your fees, but I want you to find my brother. He's all the family I've got now. I'll pay you any way I can."

I didn't know what to say; didn't like that she wanted to pay me. Whether with money or sex, I couldn't let her. It wasn't the sex or the guilt I felt for the way I used her. She made it clear she enjoyed it. But if anything had happened to Stanley, Danny would probably inherit. Like it or not, she's a suspect. Until I found if she were involved in his disappearance or not, I shouldn't get further involved—Hell! I shouldn't have spent last night. And then there's Wendy. What do I do about—another reason not to get further involved.

"I have to go. Don't worry about the fee; Carter's paying that. Where's my jacket?"

"Still in the car, I think."

"Right. I'll call you."

No POLICE CAR WAITED for me. That was a relief. I pulled out of the parking lot headed back toward the mall to catch the breakfast shift at IHOP. At the first stop sign, a police cruiser came around the corner. I watched in the rearview mirror as it parked at the motel. I turned the corner and kept going. I kept looking back, but, luckily, it didn't follow me.

Marge was retirement age, but that didn't keep her from hustling between the serving line and eight tables full of customers. She brought my breakfast: tomato juice, coffee, two eggs over medium, bacon and rye toast instead of pancakes. Have to have the rye toast.

"Sure, I know Mr. Stanley. Comes in regularly. Always orders decaf, juice, and harvest grain pancakes with sausage. No eggs. But Saturday? Let me think. Yes. He was here Saturday. Sat right over there. We greeted each other, but he wasn't my customer. Jeannie served him."

"Is she here?"

"No. She didn't come in this morning so we're short-handed. Be right back."

I ate while Marge delivered other orders and brought coffee to another new table. She worked her way back to me.

"Will there be anything else?"

"No. Breakfast was fine. Do you recall if Stanley was with anyone?"

"He was alone. He's usually alone."

"Did anything unusual occur that morning?"

"Don't think so. Clyde dropped a bunch of food and had to re-order everything, but that happens now and then."

"Did you see Stanley leave?"

"Don't think so. Why all the interest?"

"No one's seen him in several days. He seems to have disappeared right after breakfast here. Do you know how I can reach Jeannie? He may have said something to her."

"She's probably in the book. No, wait. Her name's MacPherson now. Hold on a minute."

Marge hurried away. Someone stopped her and asked something. She went to the rear of the restaurant. She came back, dropped off a fresh pot of coffee, and came to my table.

"Here. This is Jeannie's address. Don't tell where you got it. I'm not supposed to do this. It's awful that something could have happened to Mr. Stanley. He's a very nice man."

I left a good tip and an extra ten for the help. There were no police waiting and Stanley's car was still sitting where it had been since Saturday. I pulled out a map and looked up Jeannie MacPherson's street. It wasn't that far away.

The small frame house was blue-gray with white trim. It had a basement and a one-car garage in the back. There was a black conversion van with a WWJD bumper sticker parked in front of the garage. The postage stamp front yard was neatly cut with a ring of flowers around a medium-sized tree. The porch was clean. The front window drapes were closed. There was a picture of Jesus in the corner of the window. A "No Soliciting" sign hung on the screen door. I rang the bell and waited.

I caught sight of the front curtain being pulled back a bit, but no one answered the door. I rang the bell again. The door opened a crack.

"Jeannie MacPherson? Sorry to disturb you so early. I'm Rachel Cord. I'm hoping you can help me."

"We're not buying anything. Didn't you see the sign?"

"Ms. MacPherson, I'm not selling anything. I'm a private investigator."

I opened the screen door and held up my SAPI card.

"You work at the IHOP at Midtown Mall. You served a customer Saturday who's disappeared and his family is worried. I'm hoping you can help me find him. May I come in?"

The door opened a couple of inches to the extent of the safety chain so she could see my card better, but she didn't let me in. She was young, early twenties at best. She wore no make-up and her hair needed brushing. It looked like she hadn't slept well. She wore a robe that she kept tightly closed with one hand. Beneath it she wore jeans and sneakers.

"I don't know anything about a disappearance. The house is a mess. I'm not feeling too good."

"I'm sorry that you're not well." I passed her the photo of Stanley. "His name is Kenneth Stanley. You served him breakfast Saturday morning. He's a regular customer. He disappeared right after that. Anything you can tell me would be of help."

She frowned and squinted at the photo, turned her head aside briefly, before handing it back. Her nails were ragged; one was torn. There was the faintest whiff of stale urine like she hadn't bathed recently.

"I can't tell you anything. God have mercy, but I can't really help you. He ordered breakfast, ate it and left. That's all I know."

"Did anyone sit with him or speak to him?"

"No."

"Did he leave the table to use the restroom?"

"No."

"Was he okay, do you think? Was he nervous or seem upset? Did he look sick?"

"No. He was fine."

"Did he say anything to you?"

"Just hello, goodbye, stuff like that. He wondered if it was going to rain because it was clouding up. That's all. Really, I don't feel very well. I can't help you. He came in, had his breakfast, paid his bill, and left. I pray for him."

"Did you cash him out?"

She hesitated. "No. Someone else did."

"Did he leave a tip?"

"What?"

"Did he leave you a tip when he left?"

She acted like it was a trick question. Finally, "Yeah. He always leaves a tip."

"Thank you. You've been very . . ." The door closed. ". . . helpful."

Some people aren't the morning type. But she works the breakfast shift. She says she's not feeling well. Maybe she's recovering from something. Maybe Stanley's sick too and is curled up somewhere trying to recover. Sick with what? Recover where?

Stanley left the restaurant, but he never made it across the parking lot to work. What happened? Who saw him? Who took him away? Why?

I had no answers. I called Danny and told her what little I knew.

"You better call the police. The trail is getting cold. It's been five days now. Maybe there's evidence in his car or near it that I didn't see. I'm surprised it hasn't been stolen or towed."

"He's dead, isn't he?"

"We don't know that. He's missing. We don't know why. Go to the police. Make a report. Ask for Detectives Carson and Jablowski. They already know a bit about it." It'll serve them right.

"What should I tell them?"

"Everything I've told you: who I've spoken with and where to find Stanley's car. Except, please, don't suggest that I'm working for you. Tell them I'm just a friend helping out. I'm not licensed here, which is one reason I can't have you as a client. Having Carter as my client gives me some wiggle room, but I can't officially run an investigation here."

"Will you keep looking?"

"You better believe it. There are still some things I can check. But go to the police. This morning. I'll get back to you as soon as I can."

I hung up and took one last look at the MacPherson house. There was nothing unusual about it. It was like all the others around it; just a different colored pea in the pod. I saw the space in the curtain close. I started the car and headed for the river.

Eleven

THE MORNING SUN WAS shining behind me. Long shadows led me, and hundreds of others, over the river. Puffy white clouds were brilliant in the distance against the azure sky. Pockets of mist swirled along the river's edge. A boat towed three barges up the river. I noticed it all, but my mind wasn't on the scenery.

I had used Danny terribly. I did to her what Archer and Tierney had done to me. What did that make me? I wanted to blame the alcohol. I had been drunk, after all. That was no excuse. Danny had wanted it, enjoyed it. That was no excuse, either. I had relished it. What have I become? Worse, what about Wendy? How could I betray her? There were no promises or commitments between us, but it still felt like betrayal. Yes, I had been attracted to Danny, but she could be involved with Stanley's disappearance. I shouldn't have stayed. I should have taken my chances with the police. This shouldn't have happened.

You think?

Shut up.

As I came down off the bridge, I saw the police car waiting in the median beside the welcome sign. I remembered Frank's threat. Was it looking for me or checking for speeders?

I kept my speed within the limit, following traffic. I took the first off ramp, circled under the bridge, and headed south. The police car didn't follow. Time to check in with Frank.

"Hi. It's Rachel. I just listened to your messages. What's up?"

"Where the hell have you been?"

What? "I've been out of town. I'm just getting back now. What's wrong?"

"I've been trying to reach you for two days. Where are you?"

"On River Drive. In my car headed home."

"Get down here. We need to talk."

"Frank, I'm tired. I've had nearly no sleep. I need a shower. I need to change clothes. What's going on?"

"I can't talk about it on the phone. We need to see you. This is official."

"Okay, Frank. Okay. But give me a couple hours, all right? I just got in. Do I have to come in to the station, or could we meet for lunch?"

He hesitated. "Lunch is okay. Charlie's. High noon. Don't be late."

High noon? We having a shootout? What in hell was going on? Did Jablowski call Frank? Is he pissed because I went across the river again? That can't be it. He was trying to contact me before I left. What did he want? What did I do to set him off?"

I went home, threw my clothes in the hamper and took another shower. Scrubbed myself clean. At least on the outside. I fretted about what Frank wanted. Worried about what I had done to Danny. Wondered how I was going to find Stanley. What was I going to tell Wendy?

I looked at myself in the full-length mirror. The bite on my shoulder was red and forming new scabs where I washed the old ones off. Danny had drawn blood. The scratches on my back were raw also. I had two blue green hickeys on my inner thighs. There was no way I could hide all of that from

Wendy. We were supposed to have dinner and probably games later. I should call and make a rain check. Come up with some kind of an excuse.

I went to the phone and picked it up, put it down, picked it up again.

"Carter residence. Who calls, please?"

Copout!

You better believe it.

"This is Rachel Cord. Is Mr. Carter in?"

"*Si*. One moment, please."

"Rachel? This is Louise." Her voice was a little shaky. "Thank you for finding Jerry."

"You're welcome. Did he tell you what happened?"

"Yes. I think he told me everything. He said that you would be putting it all in your report. He said he was tired of hiding it."

"Are you okay?"

"Not really. I think it's disgusting. I don't know how I can ever tell the children, or explain it to my family."

"What are you going to do?"

"Get a divorce, of course. What else is there?"

"Is he there?"

"Yes. For now. We're trying to be civilized for the children. But he will be leaving soon. As soon as he can find a place. He said you're trying to find Stan. I hate that name . . . I'll have to change the boys' names. Do you need to speak with him?"

"Please. I'm sorry about all of this."

"Not your fault. When I hired you, I had no idea what you'd actually find. I never expected this. I'll get him."

There are things I hate about my job. This was one of them. Life's a bitch, but I wish it weren't.

"Rachel? Have you found Stan?"

"Not yet."

I filled him in on what I had learned and told him to expect a call from the police. There was no way to avoid it. He needed to be honest and thorough. He hadn't heard anything new or thought of any suggestions. He wanted me to keep looking and said he'd send another check.

I dressed. I chose gray and light brown plaid pants with comfortable shoes, a soft peach pullover with scoop neck, and a lightweight, light brown jacket. I changed shoulder bags, transferring everything from the one to the other.

As I left the building, I saw the condo manager and a maintenance worker staring at me. I waved and kept going. I glanced back. They were still staring. That was odd. I crossed River Drive. I looked back once more. The condo manager was walking away talking into a cell phone. The maintenance worker was still watching me.

Was I being watched? Why? Was I becoming paranoid? Or just nervous about the implied threats in Frank's messages and tone? What had I done? I picked up my pace.

I left my car because I needed to walk, even though it was going to be hot and humid. Walking is good exercise. It helps burn off excess energy and frustrations, and I was full of frustrated energy. And walking gave me time to think. I zigzagged west and north until I hit Mann Avenue by Ladies Only, my health club. I would have liked to stop and get a massage from Gretchen, but I didn't have the time. I needed to get some work done at the office before meeting Frank.

Thoughts of Wendy pestered me as I finished the twelve blocks to my office. She would be expecting a call, and we had plans, which would, hopefully, lead to fun and games. But how could I do that? I didn't want her seeing what Danny had done. We were becoming lovers. I didn't want her thinking I was a slut. Would she understand even if I didn't? Or would she walk out on me? Had I spoiled a relationship before it really began?

My office is in the west wing on the second floor of a U-shaped, old high school building. It was remodeled as an office plaza in the nineties. Mary Farr was at the circular reception desk at the top of the stairs. She and Doris Garrity provide telephone and secretarial service for several of the businesses on this second-floor wing.

"Hi, Rachel. Where you been? Haven't seen you since Monday. You have messages."

"Thanks Mary. I've been busy and out of town."

"There are two finished reports on your desk. They just need your signature before mailing. Is something going on we should know about?"

"What do you mean?"

"The police were here twice looking for you. Yesterday and again this morning."

"Here? Who?"

"A Detective Standish. Said he knew you. He left his card. Asked us to call him when you came back."

"What did he want?"

"Didn't say exactly. Asked if you had been around and if you were with anyone, particularly a woman. He showed us a picture, but we didn't know her."

What was going on? What woman?

"Anything else?"

"He wanted to see your office. We wouldn't let him. He threatened to get a warrant. We said go ahead. What's going on, Rachel?"

My question exactly. "I wish I knew."

"Ah, should I call him and say you're back?"

"Definitely. And tell him I said to go fuck himself. No. Sorry. Better not do that. He probably knows I'm back. I have a feeling I'm having lunch with him. You better call him though, so he doesn't hassle you. If I'm not out of here by twenty-to-twelve, give me a ring, okay?"

"Will do. I hope everything's all right."

"Me too."

I stomped down the hall, my footsteps echoing on the hardwood floors. Who the hell did Martin Standish think he was? He's Frank's new partner. I'd met him a few times. But asking to look at my office, that's a lot of nerve. Why were they checking on me? Had they checked with my condo manager too? Damn it to hell and back again! I hesitated before unlocking my door. I checked the lock and jamb. It didn't look like anyone had broken in. I looked down the hall. Mary was watching me. I opened the door and went in.

I turned on the lights but stayed at the door. I scanned the room. Nothing seemed out of place. My office is half of an old schoolroom. The original rooms were large with two entrances. To make affordable office space, some were divided in half by adding storage closets in the middle. The room is still large, and the tall windows provide lots of light. I get to watch great sunsets.

I've kept the schoolroom look. There's a large blackboard. In front of it is my desk, an old oak teacher's desk from the thirties. I'm sure it has lots of memories of tests and papers and shiny apples. There were two folders on the desk, probably the reports Mary mentioned, and more phone messages.

Facing the desk were six tables in two rows. I use those for separate case files. Only table one had anything on it: the file on the subpoena I served Monday before meeting Wendy. The bill for that could go out now. By the windows are two loveseats set in an L where I interview clients. At the back of the room are my storage closet and a counter with coffeepot and microwave. A small refrigerator and cabinets are beneath the counter.

I checked the closet door. It was locked. I opened it and checked my filing cabinet and safe. Both were locked. The rack of extra clothes I keep here were as they belonged. I opened the safe. My two guns were there. One was my grandfather's, a .45 caliber military semi-automatic he carried during World War II. The other was a new Smith & Wesson model 340PD, a small lightweight revolver that fires five full-load .357 Magnum rounds. Its under two-inch barrel is strictly for close range. I used one like it to kill Archer and Tierney. That one is still in an evidence room across the river even though the deaths were ruled justifiable and charges against me dropped. Carmen's still trying to get it back for me, but I wasn't holding my breath. I closed the safe.

It irked me that I was being investigated. That I couldn't understand why or have any idea what woman Standish was looking for. There was no point in dwelling on it, though; Frank would fill me in at lunch, or not. Meanwhile, I had work to catch up on.

I signed the two reports and put them in their envelopes to be mailed and filed my copies. I did the same with the subpoena I served, filling in the date and time on the form. I went through my messages. There were four from Frank. I tossed them in the trash. There was one from PJs from yesterday: "Thursday is meatball and spaghetti night. We eat at 5 p.m.; don't be a stranger."

PJs is a widowed grandmother who takes in runaways to her large home in Lincoln Heights. The police killed her husband years ago accidentally. A large settlement and a hands-off attitude by the city lets PJs run her home for runaways without social services or police intervention. While she was recovering from her husband's death, PJs began wearing his pajamas all the time. Even now pajamas are all she wears: all styles, all makes. That and fuzzy slippers. PJs is the queen of pajamas, and one of my best contacts for finding the runaways I'm hired to locate. It was PJs and two of her granddaughters who helped me back in May when I was raped. Rasheena and Shoshana stayed with me for several weeks as I recovered from that ordeal.

Another message was from a Mavis Webb who called on Monday and wanted to hire me. When it rains, it pours—third client in a week. The last message was from Captain Rodecker: "Call me." He had called this morning.

Captain Rodney Roderick Rodecker III was Carson and Jabba's boss. He was also an old friend. We served together as MPs in Saudi Arabia and Kuwait during the first Gulf War. Jabba calls him "Hot Rod" because he's young, still new to their force, and already a captain. I knew him as "Hot Rod" because of the randy reputation he earned in the Gulf that had nothing to do with any of his three names. Carson and Jabba must have filled him in. I knew I'd have to call him.

I chickened and called Mavis Webb instead.

"Ms. Webb? This is Rachel Cord returning your call. I've been away on a case. How may I help you?"

"It's Mrs. Webb, and you can catch my cheatin' husband doin' the dirty with his secretary. That's how you can help me."

"I see. My workload is heavy at the moment. We could meet next week. Or I could recommend another agency."

"Oh, no. You're the best. You done great the last time. If I have to wait to chop his thing off, I'll wait. I want you."

Last time? I looked again at her name on the message.

"I'm sorry. I don't recall your name. I've worked for you before?"

"No. No. I used to be Mavis Brown. You worked for my husband's ex, Clovia. Four years ago."

Mavis Brown? Clovia Webb? Clarence Webb!

"Now I remember. *You* were the secretary."

"That's right. That's how I know you're good. We were real careful. Well, I married the cheatin' bastard. I should have known better. Clovia ran him through the wringer with the stuff you got. Now I want the same. I'm even usin' her lawyer."

"Would Monday at 2:00 PM. be all right? At my office?"

"Monday's Labor Day; we have plans. Could we meet Tuesday?

"That's fine; Tuesday at two. I'm in the Mann Avenue Plaza, West Wing, Room 222. See you Tuesday."

Clarence Webb was a CPA. I had been hired to see if he was fooling around and to get evidence if he were. I went to see him in a slightly tarty outfit to see how he reacted, see if he were really the fooling around type or if my client were just paranoid. Webb was practically all over me. His secretary,

Mavis, was livid. I was sure they were doing it, and it wasn't that hard to prove. I don't know what Mavis thinks "real careful" is, but the office couch and the motel down the street doesn't do it for me.

I remembered that Clarence was tight with a nickel and a creature of habit. Was it possible he was "doin' the dirty" with his new secretary on that same couch? And did he still have a free room in exchange for his accounting services at that same motel he had used with Mavis? If so, I'd be able to get the proof quickly.

I wrote down the appointment with Mavis and decided to bite the bullet and call Rod. My phone rang first.

"Hey, tits for brains; it's Jablowski. Thanks for nothing. Your girlfriend's filled us in. We got stuck with the case."

"Congratulations. If you haven't flushed your brains down the toilet yet this morning, maybe you'll find her brother."

"Yeah, well it might help if we had the keys to his house and a copy of that photo you were waving around. Save us some time and having to break in."

"Shit. They're still in my bag."

"Why am I not surprised? So stuff your balloons back in the car and hustle them over here. Then, as Paul Harvey used to say, you can tell us the rest of the story."

"I can't get there before three."

"Make it two."

"I can't—"

"You rather we have you arrested for impeding an investigation?"

"Okay. I'll be there."

"Thought so. You phony dicks give me a pain."

I wasn't sure if he meant my being a PI or was referring to my being a lesbian. It didn't matter. Guess I didn't need to call Rod after all. How could I have been so stupid as to have not left the keys with Danny? Because she's a suspect, like it or not.

The shit was piling. I needed to move the outhouse. I looked at my desk planner. My survival group would meet next week, and I would see Dr. Howard on the 14th. Would she see me sooner? I should talk to someone. What about Frank? I could always talk to him before, but can I trust him now? I hate being dependent. And Wendy? Can I talk to Wendy? I can work through this. I'm an intelligent adult. I am. Maybe I should go to spaghetti night if I get back in time. I haven't seen PJs or her granddaughters in weeks. Maybe she could help straighten my head.

I took out two new single-subject notebooks and a stack of 3x5 index cards. I got a diet soda from the fridge. I put one notebook on table five and sat at table three with the other and the notepad I carry with me. I sat with my hands folded on the table staring at the blank blackboard, trying to put my personal issues aside. I let myself relax — went back to school. This is how I work.

I think of each case as a research paper. Gathering data. Putting it together. The notebooks are running commentary, everything as I find it. The index cards are for key points: items of interest and questions and answers. I can sort these in any order, lay them out like a jigsaw puzzle; see relationships I might have overlooked. Fill in holes with more questions to be asked. Each case gets its own table. Sometimes I'll use the blackboard for lists or to work out a problem.

I completed my notebook on Carter, drafted a report for Louise and was finishing my notes on Stanley at table five. I had just written on an index card, "Was Jeannie MacPherson watching from the window or was it someone else? Why?" when the phone rang.

"It's twenty-to-twelve."

"Thanks, Mary."

I straightened the desk files, double-checked that everything that should be was locked, grabbed my bag and left. I gave Mary the billing information on the subpoena, the two reports to mail, and told her about the appointment for

Tuesday.

"I probably won't be back today. Seeya."

Twelve

IT'S A SEVEN BLOCK WALK to Charlie's Chicago Hot Dog Stand on the corner of Cutter Avenue and Central Boulevard. Charlie's Chicago dog is exceptional: a toasted poppy seed bun and an over-sized all-beef hot dog covered with yellow mustard, onions, chopped fresh cucumber, neon green relish, tomato wedges, Greek peppers and a dash of celery salt. Main course and salad all in one: a work of art and a delight to the senses. Well, that's the way it should be.

My late experience with Archer and, especially, Tierney, turned me off hot dogs and I haven't gotten my desire back. I've come close a couple times, eating everything but the dog. At least now I can watch someone else eat them without turning my head or gagging. Which makes it better for Frank. Because for Frank Taylor, they're a bit of heaven. And a reminder of home. Frank was a Chicago cop for years before family illness brought him here. He still misses the Cubs and Sox home games, but he never misses his daily hot dog.

As I expected, Martin Standish was with him at the picnic table under the oak. Frank had his usual two dogs in front of him. Marty was eating plain French fries and coleslaw. Marty doesn't eat hot dogs or any meat that I know of. I've wondered how long their partnership would last.

I went to the window and got an order of chili fries and a diet soda. I sat across from them. Frank hadn't touched his dogs. That was unusual. Actually, that was unheard of. What had I done?

"Okay, Frank. What's the problem, and what was Marty doing at my office?"

Frank is a big chocolate bear. He looks soft and cuddly, but there's a lot of tough muscle and sinew beneath the surface. Right now he looked grumpy.

"That's hard to say, Rachel. Where you been?"

"I told you on the phone. I've been out of town, working."

"Who was the woman at your apartment?" Marty asked.

"What?"

"Who was the woman at your apartment, if you've been out of town?"

"None of your business. Did you ask about me at my condo? Frank? What the hell is going on?"

"Just answer the question, Rachel." Frank's tone was dead serious.

"Is this her?"

Marty placed a blow-up driver's license photo of my ex-lover, Karen Tanaka, on the table.

"Frank. You know damn well I haven't seen Karen in . . ."

I stopped. I looked back at the photo. I held it. It was Karen, but it wasn't Karen. The resemblance was uncanny. What was going on? Who was this?

"I don't know this woman. I've never met her."

"What about her." Marty put another photo on the table.

It was grainy, a bit blurry and the baseball cap didn't help. The picture looked like it was taken from a security camera videotape. It was a woman walking across a parking lot. It could have been the same woman. It could have been Karen. There was a time/date in the corner: "0745-08/28." Last Saturday. Was Karen back? Why hadn't she contacted me?

"Rachel, is this Karen Tanaka?" Frank pointed to the security photo. "Have you seen her?"

"No, I haven't seen Karen. I don't know. This looks like her, but it looks like that other woman too."

Karen, where are you? Why are the police looking for you? Who is this other woman that looks like you? Why did you leave me? Are you coming home?

"Is this the woman staying in your apartment?" Marty persisted.

"No one's staying at my place except me."

"Then who was there Monday and stayed there Tuesday night?"

"What? How do you . . .? How dare you! You've got no fucking business talking to my neighbors."

"Rachel!" Frank said. "Rachel. Calm yourself. It is our business. This is a homicide investigation."

Homicide?

"I'm lost, Frank. What are you talking about?"

Frank looked down at his hot dogs. They were getting cold. He seemed to be praying. Marty glared at me. I always thought there was a bit of weasel behind his sandy hair and freckles. Frank took a bite of dog—not enjoying it—but using it to take his time, deciding how much he was going to tell me. I relaxed, taking slow deep breaths. I ignored any interest Marty might have in the rise and fall of my bosom. Fuck him! I sipped my soda.

"Early Saturday morning," Frank said, "after dawn, a fisherman walking along the river thought he saw someone doing some illegal dumping. This was above North Ferry, just inside the city line. It was a woman. He yelled at her. She drove away before he could get close. However, he did get the license number and found what she was dumping: a contractor's-sized trash bag half buried in a deep hole. He was curious and opened the bag. Actually it was two bags one inside the other. A hand flopped out. It took him a while to get to a phone and call the police. He showed them the bag and described the car and the woman he saw. The woman was Oriental, about five-six, light framed with dark hair in a ponytail. Age undetermined. She was wearing dark-colored jeans, black or blue, a gray sweatshirt and a baseball cap."

I looked at the security photo again. It was the same woman, but was it Karen? Frank ate another bite of hot dog before continuing. Marty didn't look happy about Frank telling me so much. They probably argued about how they were going to handle it before I arrived, but Frank was the senior partner.

"The officers put a call out on the car. They secured the scene and waited for Forensics and Detectives Montero and Lockhart to arrive."

I knew Ed Montero and Dean Lockhart. They worked the gay beatings case that resulted in the death of Sarah Hastings. They worked out of City Central now.

"A patrol found the car at Westbrook Mall late Saturday night. A check of security cameras produced that photo. The car belonged to Aiko Nagasawa. That's her there." Frank pointed to the driver's photo. "The DMV had already provided that information. Miss Nagasawa wasn't at her apartment. The apartment manager said that she left a note for him sometime Friday night saying she was going out of town on a trip. He didn't speak to her."

"Then why are you looking for Karen, if you want this other woman?"

"Because the body found at the river was Aiko Nagasawa. And according to the medical examiner, she was killed sometime Friday afternoon or evening. She couldn't have left the note for the manager, and that's definitely not her walking across the parking lot."

A chill ran up my back. The short hairs on my neck bristled. I looked at the surveillance photo again.

"Frank, this can't be Karen. It can't be. Karen couldn't murder anyone. Besides, she's been gone for a year; left the state, as I've told you often enough. What makes you think this is her?"

"The same reasons you just did. I didn't know Karen that well except through you. She was at my house a few times with you, and Lorraine and I went to one of her art shows. Do you think I wouldn't think of her when copies of those photos hit my desk?"

"No, of course you would have. But I'm telling you, it's not Karen. It can't be."

It can't be.

"Maybe, maybe not. After I saw these, I got an old staff photo from Cramer College to show the fisherman. He says it looks like the woman he saw. Do you know where Karen is now?"

"Still in Florida as far as I know."

"When did you last talk to her?"

"Frank, I haven't seen or heard from Karen since she ran out on me a year ago. I've moped and cried on your shoulder enough for you to remember that."

"She hasn't tried to contact you recently? You're sure she's in Florida?"

"No, she hasn't contacted me. No, I don't *know* that she's still in Florida. I traced her there last November. My last letter came back after New Year marked 'no longer at this address/no forwarding address.' I haven't gotten a hit on her since. To be accurate, I've no idea where she is."

"So she could be here."

"Yes, she could be, I suppose. But if she is, she hasn't contacted me. Frank, you haven't treated me like this since we first met—when I caught that cop wannabe."

"Sorry, Rachel, but this is a murder investigation, and we need to know that Karen isn't involved."

"So who was the woman in your apartment? Did you help this Tanaka woman get out of the area?"

"Marty, you're really annoying. Do you know that?"

"What I know is that your lover may be involved in this murder. That some woman, who may be her, was in your apartment Monday and Tuesday possibly hiding. That you've been avoiding us and not returning calls. That you conveniently left town and didn't tell anyone where you were going. Maybe you sneaked her out of state. That's what I know, and I don't like it."

"First of all, I really don't care what you like. Who visits me is my business. It wasn't Karen. I wasn't avoiding anyone. Secondly, I have a bad habit of not always checking messages or leaving my phone on. Sorry about that. I didn't 'conveniently leave town,' I have clients, and I was working. Lastly, I'm my own boss. I don't have to check in."

Read between the lines, asshole.

Frank intervened. They asked more questions. I confirmed that Karen had taught art at Cramer College; her sudden resignation and departure surprised the college as much as it had me. Karen was originally from California. I gave them the address I had in Florida and told Frank I'd get him Karen's family's address and names and addresses of her other friends I knew.

I didn't think it would do any good. I checked with everyone several times after Karen left. No one else heard from her either. I would check again though. If Karen was back, I wanted to know it. If she was in any way involved with this murder, I wanted to know that too.

I left Frank and Marty sitting at the table. Frank hadn't eaten his second hot dog. I tossed my fries and soda in the trash and hurried away. I didn't care what they might be thinking of my actions. I was going to be hard pressed to get to Rod's office on time.

I turned on my cell phone and checked my voicemail. There was one message from Wendy.

"Hi, are you back yet? There's a picture of Karen in today's paper. Have you seen it? What's going on? Call me."

I wasn't ready to call Wendy. Wasn't sure what I was going to say. I passed a newsstand and grabbed a paper. Aiko Nagasawa's picture was on the front page under the headline

"Have you seen this woman?" Her name wasn't listed. Anyone with information on the woman or someone looking like her was asked to call the police. No other details were given. The security camera photo was on an inside page.

Karen, you better not be involved.

Thirteen

I WAITED ON A HARD BENCH in the squad room. Carson and Jabba had been in Rodecker's office with the blinds closed for 30 minutes. They were probably playing liar's poker or something, letting me stew. The other detectives and officers would look at me occasionally out of the corners of their eyes and grin. I was 10 minutes late arriving and the desk sergeant downstairs had said, "Five more minutes, and we were supposed to arrest you. Better get upstairs."

"Excuse me," said the woman next to me. She was handcuffed to the arm of the bench. She pointed to my breasts.

"May I ask where you got those? Were they expensive?"

Her makeup was strictly nighttime, overdone for this time of day. She was small-breasted—how lucky—and wore a strapless black knit sheath that hugged her body and stopped only inches below her crotch. It was some kind of easy-care miracle fabric, strictly wash and wear.

"I grew them myself, and they're as expensive as hell. If you want them, maybe we could arrange a transplant exchange."

"They can do that?"

"Honey, nowadays they can do anything. Gotta go."

Carson had come out of the office and motioned me over.

I wondered whom Rod would send out to get me, Nice or Nasty. I knew I was in deep, but maybe the kimchi wasn't over my head yet.

As we entered the office, I made a goodwill gesture by putting the keys to Stanley's house and his picture on the desk.

"Sorry. I forgot to leave these with Danny. If that's all you need—"

"Sit down."

Rod wasn't pleased. Just what I needed: two police forces on my case.

We sat for several moments in silence, the three of them staring at me. I stared at the photo of Rod's family. Wife and three children. The boy's name was Michael, the girls, Melissa and Morgan. No more Triple-Rs in Rod's family tree. The wait felt like hours. Rod leaned forward.

"For the sake of old friendships, and the wonderful times we've all shared, why don't you tell us everything you know about Kenneth Stanley's disappearance?"

That hurt. I wasn't sure how much they knew. I could do some lying, but lies tend to come back to bite you. At least they do me. The truth is easier to remember. I told them pretty much everything, even about peeing myself outside the garage. Adding something embarassing gives the impression of total honesty. If Forensics needed to go out there, they would most likely find the spot anyway. I left out details of my time with and shortness of relationship with Danny, and that I had made a video copy.

"So," Rod asked, "Miss Steele hired you to find her brother?"

"No. She's just a friend. I didn't realize they were brother and sister until later. Besides, I can't accept clients over here, as you well know. I'm working for Carter. He lives on my side of the river."

"But he hired you over here," Jabba said.

"I'll let my lawyer argue that, if necessary. I just want to find Stanley."

"So do we, now." Rod said. "But it's been five days. That doesn't make it easier."

"I only found out yesterday. Was there anything useful in his car?"

"We don't think so. We impounded it to check further, but I doubt there'll be anything. Do you think your client could be involved?"

"Don't see how. I told you how I found him. Couple more days, he may have been dead."

"What about the sister?"

"Honestly? I don't know. I like her, so I don't want to believe she's involved; but she does stand to gain from Stanley's death. If he's dead, that is."

"Yeah, we know how much you like her," Jabba said. "You spent the night with her."

I glared at him. Rod continued.

"We're checking her out. Now go home, Rachel. Leave this to us. As much as we love having you around, stay on your side of the river."

I sat in the car, holding my keys, deciding what to do next. Rod was right. It was their business now. But I like to earn my money, and I don't like being brushed aside. Maybe that's why I made a new house key and copied Stanley's photo before coming over the river. I didn't need to go back to Stanley's right away. Not before the police had a thorough chance at the place anyway. But I might have missed something, and someone would have to check on Amber in a day or so. I called Danny.

"Hey, Cowgirl. You comin' back for another ride?"

My cheeks burned. "Don't think so. I just left the police. They want me to stay out of this. There's no sign of your brother yet. They're checking you out."

"Thought they might. That's not a problem. I was in some trouble years back out in San Francisco, but nothing since. I had nothing to do with whatever happened to Kenny. I've got solid alibis for my time here. I hope you'll keep looking for him. I trust you more than I do the cops."

"I'll keep looking. That's what Carter's paying me to do. There are still some leads I can track down."

"Thanks. I'm glad you're staying with it. I wish I could afford to pay you too. You sure you don't want another ride? I didn't think you were the one-night type."

I'm not, but . . . "I'll stay in touch."

My involvement with Danny was a mistake.

You think?

Shut up. But there wasn't much I could do about what happened; just try to not let it happen again. Time to bite the bullet. I called Wendy.

"Hi. I wondered when you'd call. Are we still getting together tonight?"

"Yes. I need to see you. Would eight be okay?"

"If we have to wait that long, that's fine. Should I bring some wine?"

"There's Chardonnay in the fridge."

"That'll work. Have you seen the paper? Were those pictures of Karen?"

"No, it wasn't Karen. I'll tell you about that too."

"All right. See you tonight."

It couldn't be Karen.

Why not?

Because Karen's in Florida. Because Karen's not a murderer. Because I lived with her for three years. Because I believe in her. Because I still love her. That's why not.

Rush hour over the bridge was a crawl, a bumper-to-bumper parking lot. I thought all the commuters worked in my town. I made another call.

"Gainesville Police Department. How may I direct your call?"

"Detective Helen Abernathy, please."

"One moment, please."

Helen Abernathy — the African Queen — another memory

from the Gulf War. Once the toughest, sassiest MP captain in the Army, and the best commander any soldier could want. Too bad she wasn't bent my way. Now a cop in Florida and still a friend.

"This is Detective Abernathy. How may I help you?"

"Helen. It's Rachel Cord. How are you?"

"Rachel. Haven't heard from you in months. We're doing fine if Frances doesn't blow us away. What about you? You still playing Mike Hammer?"

"I'm more Christy Love. Who's Frances?"

"Hurricane Frances. Don't you watch the news?"

"Not if I can avoid it. It's always bad. I have enough of that of my own. The reason I called, do you remember Karen Tanaka?"

"The woman you had me go see? Yes, I remember her. Are you still carrying the torch?"

"No. It went out." Liar. "But I need to know if she's still in Florida." I told Helen what Frank had told me. "That's why I need to find her. I don't believe she's involved in any way, but I expect the police here will contact your department with an official request for information."

"I'll do what I can, unofficially, but don't expect too much."

"I just need to know that she's still there. Or when she left and where to, if you can find out."

"I'll try to get what I can today. If Frances hits here like expected, it's going to be a mess this weekend. There will probably be a lot of power outages. I have to tell you, though, that that look-alike business is odd. One, I might accept, but two is a stretch, and you know it."

"I realize that, but what else could it be? Karen couldn't kill anyone, so it has to be a third person who looks like her."

"I know you feel that way, although, frankly, I don't know what you saw in that woman."

"What do you mean? Karen was the sweetest person I've ever known."

"If you say so. Maybe she changed. Remember, she walked out on you. When I saw her, she was very cold and aloof. Nervous, too. Made me think she was hiding something. Maybe she just doesn't like cops or was mad that you sent me to find her."

"That's probably it."

"Look, don't be a stranger. Come down for a visit some time if we don't get blown away."

"I will. And thanks, Helen."

I finally made it back to the office. Mary and Doris were gone; most of the other offices were closed. I pulled out the file on Karen from the locked cabinet in the closet and sat with it on the loveseat. I thought I was done with this stuff. Thought I was done with the heartache. Far from it. I went through the file quickly and called Frank with the information he wanted.

"Thanks, Rachel. I know this is hard on you. Why did you go back across the river after lunch?"

"Did you follow me? I thought we were friends."

"We are, but Karen may be a suspect in a murder investigation. Don't take it personally. It's part of the job."

"But it is personal. Karen didn't kill anyone. And you can check with *your* friend Jablowski as to what I was doing. I was with him and Rodecker on another matter."

"Wayne's a good guy, a good cop. So you really haven't seen Karen?"

"No, Frank. As I've told you several times, I haven't seen Karen. I wish I had though. Frank, we're friends. Why do you think I would lie to you?"

"Because it's Karen."

I had no answer to that.

"She's not involved, Frank. I know she's not involved."

"I hope you're right."

Me too. More than you know. There wasn't much else to say.

"Tell me, is Wayne a first or middle name?"

"Why?"

"Just curious."

I called Karen's old friends and colleagues. Most had seen the paper or watched the news. They hadn't seen or heard from Karen since she left. They were as amazed as I was by the resemblance. They wanted to know if they should call the police. I said they could but that the police would be contacting them. I called Karen's sister, Tori, in southern California. No news there, either.

I went through the file again. Karen left a year ago. The week I was in San Francisco on business. We had had a stupid fight.

"You're going to stay with that woman, aren't you?"

"Yes. It'll save on expenses. Carrie's an old friend."

"Old lover you mean."

"Carrie and I had a brief affair in basic training. That was ages ago. Nothing's going to happen. Karen, I love you. Only you. Come here."

But made up before I left.

"I'm sorry for being jealous."

"Come with me."

"Wish I could, but this isn't a good time."

I called her several times and flirted over the phone. She seemed to miss me and want me home. I told her again that she should have come along, but it was too close to the fall semester starting for her to leave. Everything seemed fine. That was the last time I spoke with her.

When I came back, she and many of her things were gone. Whatever would fit in her car, apparently. She left no note. Nothing. I tried calling her, but her cell phone was turned off. I found out later that she had stopped her mail.

I reviewed the one credit card statement in her file that had been delivered by mistake. It had helped me track her. Gas purchases, fast-food places, motels.

She bought gas and food in Indianapolis. Stayed the night in Nashville, more gas and food. That was a big loop. What was she doing? Where was she going? Gas again in Asheville, NC. Two nights in Wilmington, NC. Gas in Columbia, SC. Gas and food in Atlanta. Gas in Meridian, MS. A week's stay in New Orleans. She was all over the map. Gas in Pensacola and Gainesville, FL; a week in a motel in Gainesville, then a utility bill and groceries. She finally settled. That's where Helen found her.

I looked at the last credit report I ran on her in April. There was a flurry of activity in November after Helen saw her leaving maxed out credit cards now in serious arrears. Non payment of a loan. Bank overdrawn, bounced checks. Then nothing. No further activity. What happened, Karen? That wasn't like you. You were always on top of things, better organized. Why did you flip out? Was it me?

I couldn't merge the woman I saw on paper with the woman I had loved and lived with. My vision didn't jibe with the image Frank was seeing. It didn't make any sense. I flipped through my stack of index cards, trying to form a pattern, trying to see something I hadn't seen before. There was just a large hole and nothing to fill it.

Karen, if you're here, call me. I can help you.

"AND THERE ARE TWO other banks besides ours that can lower your current rate. You're not eating. The kung pao too spicy?"

I looked up at Wendy. "No. It's fine. Everything tastes great." Not like the mess I've made. "I'm just not hungry, I guess." And you look wonderful, and now I'm going to make a bigger mess.

"I guess this isn't the best time to discuss refinancing your mortgage. You're worried about Karen, aren't you?"

"Yes." That too. "I thought I was over her, but now that she may be back, I feel the same way again, and she may be in trouble. I want to help her, but the thing is, I may . . ." also love you, but I cheated on you last night and if I tell you, I know you'll hate me, but if I don't tell you then I'm still cheating, and . . . "I'm very confused."

"I would think so. One woman who looks like Karen is murdered, and another one who looks like her may be the murderer? I find that very confusing."

"It's not just that."

I need to tell you what happened last night, but I'm scared.

"Is it this other case you told me about? That seems pretty weird too."

"Wendy . . ."

I want to hold you, love you, but I can't. How can I? Do you know that I'm falling in love with you? That I don't deserve you.

Wendy got up and started around the table. I was afraid to let her touch me, afraid that I would break down, afraid that . . . just so afraid. I moved away to the living room, went to the balcony doors. Stared out into the darkness. I could see her behind me in the glass, coming to me. Stay away! I'm unclean! She put her hands on top of my shoulders, squeezed and massaged my shoulders and neck with her wonderful hands. Trying to take the tension from me, yet leaving me even tenser. She wrapped her arms around me. I felt her warm breath on my neck, her kiss.

"It's all right. Whatever it is. There's something else I want to discuss tonight. An idea I came up with. This might not be the best time to suggest it. It's too soon, I know. It's sort of crazy, really, but . . . I know how you felt—feel—about Karen. I understand that, and I'm sure all this mistaken identity stuff will work itself out. And you'll find that Stanley guy. It'll all be all right."

"No, it won't." God! I'm going to lose you. "Wendy . . ."

"This is hard for me, Rachel. We've known each other for such a short time. There's such an age difference . . . After Nancy . . . I shouldn't rush things, but I want you to consider, to think about . . . my . . . idea . . . that is . . ."

I knew she'd walk out on me if I told her about Danny,

about what I had done. I only half listened to what she was trying to say. I was too afraid to tell her what I *had* to tell her; yet keeping it hidden was killing me too. We hadn't made any promises; this thing of ours was too new. And yet . . . I knew it would hurt her. Didn't want to hurt her.

Wendy held me. I wished time would stop at that very moment and never move forward. But if wishes were horses, then we'd all be up to our necks in . . .

"Wendy?"

How can I do this? How can I not?

"Anyway, what I'm trying to suggest . . . Yes?"

She hugged me. Tears filled my eyes.

"Last night. Last night when I didn't come home."

"Yes? What about it?"

"Something terrible happened."

Was it this hard for Carter when he told Louise the truth? Will the truth truly set me free?

"I . . . I . . ."

Wendy massaged my neck. "What happened? You can tell me."

"I slept with another woman."

She froze, her fingers stiff on my shoulders.

"What?

She moved away from me.

"You what?"

I turned. "I slept with another woman. I didn't mean for it to happen. Please forgive me."

She shook her head in disbelief. "No. No, I don't believe it. Is this some sort of test? A joke? It's not funny if it is."

"It's not a joke. I'm sorry. I really didn't mean for it to happen. I wanted to be here with you last night. Really. You have to believe that. But I was working. I had to follow up on some leads to find Stanley. The thing is, I got drunk—which is no excuse, I know—and the police were watching me, and Danny asked me to stay so they couldn't arrest me for DUI, and—Danny's Stanley's sister—and somehow we, that is—"

120

"I don't want to hear it. I—Do—Not—Want—To—Hear—Your—Excuses."

Wendy turned and walked away. She turned back.

"How could you? I thought . . . We made love the night before last. Woke up yesterday morning in each other's arms—Yesterday morning—and last night you . . . We made plans to be together again. I thought tonight would . . . Do you know that I was going to suggest . . . to ask if I could move . . . and you went off and . . . How could you sleep . . .? You bitch."

"Wendy, please don't leave. Let me explain. Wendy, please"—the door slammed—"don't go."

Fourteen

Flames blazed as I poked at the sticks in the fire ring. I felt the heat, but they failed to warm me in the cool morning air. The tips of the buildings of my city across the river turned red, then gold, shining in the early morning light. It promised to be a beautiful day, but not for me.

Gray mist softly rose as the mud-black river churned and rolled mindlessly along its way. I wanted to float away in that mindless flow, forget every ugly thing that happened, that I had done. Disappear as if I had never been. I pulled Danny's fringed jacket tightly around me and contemplated how stupid I was.

After Wendy left, I repeatedly called her cell phone to beg her forgiveness, but she wouldn't answer. Later, she must have turned it off because all I got was a message saying the phone was out of service. I left messages each time, trying to explain what happened, trying to tell her how I felt about her. Then I called her home phone; left messages there when no one answered. The fourth time, Clare answered.

"Rachel, Wendy won't speak with you. She's not speaking to me, either, right now."

"Clare, I—"

"You don't need to explain. From your messages, I can

guess what happened. It's too bad, really. Right now she's very upset, very hurt."

"I didn't want to hurt her, but I had to tell her."

"I know, but your timing was terrible. Rachel, Wendy . . . Wendy is a banker. A conservative—very conservative—banker. She doesn't do things on whim or impulse; at least not since Nancy. You changed that. This is the most excited I've seen her in years. She was so looking forward to tonight. She told me she was going to surprise you with, in her words, 'a bold, audacious suggestion.'"

"I don't understand."

"I'm trying to explain, but I don't know if it's my place to do so. Wendy wouldn't want me to say anything, especially now. But . . . you're my friend, a survivor sister. Wendy's my daughter. I love you both. I want the best for each of you. Over the past months, as I've grown to know you, I thought you were someone that Wendy would like. That's why I arranged for you to meet occasionally. I hoped that something would happen, would spark, between she and you. I didn't expect the whirlwind of this week; and, I didn't expect what happened tonight."

"I still don't quite get what you're trying to tell me."

"It's difficult. Wendy would think I betrayed her if I tell, but . . . Wendy was going to suggest that she move in with you."

"What? She . . . with me?" Oh, god.

"Yes. She was going to suggest it as a financial arrangement, but I know that she wanted it to be much, much more."

"I blew it. That would have . . . I really blew it."

"Perhaps, perhaps not. Give her some time, Rachel. I hope you two work this out, but please don't call again tonight. Thank you."

Wendy wanted to move in with me. A mindblower. And I did what I did without consideration, without thought. I hurt her. I was crap. Worse than crap. I drowned myself in

Glenfiddich, but it tasted wrong, wasted; thought of losing myself in Margo's voice, but it was hours before I could call him. In the end, before I was too drunk to drive, I ran to Danny.

I used Danny. Came skulking in the night seeking penance. Made her punish me for the whore, slut, bitch I was. Used her to purge me, if that were possible. We clutched and clawed and ravished each other. She didn't care why I was there, only that I was. Maybe I was no different than Carter.

I was sore, bruised and scratched; but our actions didn't take away the ache, the shame of what I had done. I had hurt Wendy. Coming here didn't fix that. Solved nothing. At best, it made things worse. I poked at the ashes, at the dying flames.

I climbed the stairs from the river and went to my car; held my keys but didn't open the door. I went to Danny's room.

She lay on her stomach, uncovered, her head buried beneath the pillow. I put her jacket on a chair. She peeked out at me.

"You get up way too early."

"I have to leave."

Danny struggled up; hugged one bent leg to her and stared at me through the shadowed light.

"You're not coming back, are you?"

"Not for this. This isn't for me. Your passions are too extreme. It's not what I really want. Who I want. I'm sorry."

"Do you love that woman?"

"Which one? The one I can't find who I thought I knew but may be a murderer, or the one I've hurt by being with you and chased away? At this point, I don't really know."

"You're a rough rider, Rachel Cord. If they don't want you, I'll still be here."

"I'm sorry I've hurt you too. I'll call when I get news of your brother."

Fifteen

THE DOORBELL AND THE banging woke me. It was only 11:30. Late morning light through the drapes turned my bedroom a cool blue. It took me a moment to focus. I came home straight from Danny's and went to bed. It was too early for anything else. My clothes were in a pile on the floor. Someone was hammering on my front door.

"I'm coming. I'm coming! Hold on!"

I wrapped my robe around me. Frank Taylor filled the peephole and pounded on the door again. I opened it.

"You don't have to knock it down."

Frank pushed past me followed by Detectives Ed Montero, Dean Lockhart and Martin Standish.

"Well, just barge on in, why don't you."

Standish and Lockhart headed for the bedrooms.

"Hey! You can't go in there."

"Yes, we can," Montero said handing me a search warrant.

"What is this all about?"

"Murder, Miss Cord."

Montero was being very formal, but then, we weren't the best of friends.

"Well, I haven't murdered anyone, lately."

"That's good to know. Where do you keep your gun?"

"Why? Afraid I might shoot you?"

"Yes. Where is it?"

"In a safe at my office. I don't keep guns at home."

Standish and Lockhart came back into the room. "She's alone." "No one else here." I looked around for Frank. He was in the kitchen.

"Frank, what are you doing?"

"Making coffee. Why don't you get dressed?"

What did they want? I hurried into bra, panties, jeans and sweatshirt, and brushed my hair. What did the warrant say? Should I call Carmen?

They were all sitting at the dining table drinking coffee when I came back into the room. There was a cup for me at the head of the table. I could see that there was another pot brewing. Great. Should I break out the cookies?

"Did I forget I invited everyone over for breakfast?"

"Sit down," Montero said.

"Should I call my lawyer?"

"You can, if you want. But that won't stop us from tearing the place apart before she gets here."

Standish looked eager to do just that.

"And if I cooperate?"

"Then we probably won't have to tear things apart to find what we need."

I sat down. "Would someone tell me what's going on that brings four detectives into my home?"

"Rachel," Frank said, "it's important that we locate Karen Tanaka. Marty and I are here because I made the Tanaka connection, and because we're your friends."

I glanced at Standish. He didn't look like a friend.

"That doesn't tell me what's going on. What Tanaka connection?"

"How long have you known Karen Tanaka?" Lockhart asked.

"We lived together for three years. I haven't seen her in a

year. Frank? What Tanaka connection?"

"Why are you going across the river?" Standish asked. "Who was the woman you had here?"

"You're a broken record, Marty. I'm working a missing person case, and I told you, who I have here is none of your business."

"It's our business, if we say it is."

"The hell it is."

"There are more bodies."

Everything stopped. Montero's words echoed in my head. More bodies? Everything seemed frozen. Whose?

"When did you first meet Tanaka?" Lockhart asked.

"I . . ." Bodies? "That is . . . ah . . . we first met when that cop wannabe murdered those students in College Park. Karen taught Art at Cramer College; two of the women were her students. We met again and dated six or eight months before we moved in together. Frank? What bodies? Do you think Karen . . ."

I couldn't say it, refused to think it.

"Tanaka came here from San Mateo, California, is that right?" Lockhart asked.

"Yes. You think Karen . . . killed someone else? Frank?"

Frank reached across and held my hand. "Another body was found buried near where Aiko Nagasawa was found. It's been there at least two years, maybe longer. We don't know who it is yet. But she was Oriental with dark hair and about the same size."

I looked at Montero. "You said bodies."

"Six years ago, in San Mateo, Evelyn Martinez, a Japanese-Mexican-American woman disappeared. No one knew why she left or where she went. Two years later her body was identified as one found buried in doubled trash bags in an out-of-the-way area. Just like Nagasawa and the new body we've found. An ex-boyfriend was suspected at the time but never charged."

"What does that have to do with Karen?"

Montero laid a photograph on the table. It was a blow-up from a driver's license ID. Looking at her, no one would have guessed she was part Hispanic. She looked very Japanese. She looked very much like Karen.

"From the information you gave me," Frank said, "I queried San Mateo about Karen. The detective who worked the Martinez case saw the photo we sent. She contacted us this morning."

"I know what you're thinking, but Karen didn't do that. And she didn't kill Naga-what's-her-name or that other woman. She's not a murderer. She's not. She's in Florida."

"No, she's not. I also received a reply from my query to Gainesville, Florida. It came back more quickly than I expected. It was like they had the information already waiting. Karen Tanaka was last seen there in mid-November. She ran out on her lease and local bills, left all of her belongings, and sold her car to a used car dealer in Jacksonville. Then she disappeared again. I alerted the police there to check for any missing person reports involving Japanese-American women. There may be a body there too."

"We think she came back here," Montero said. "When and why, we don't know. We think she killed Aiko Nagasawa, the unidentified woman, and the Martinez woman in California. We're looking to see if there are any other bodies to be found. We need to find her. California also wants to talk with her."

If they were still talking, I didn't hear them. I tried to absorb what I had already heard, tried to resolve conflicts in my mind. Karen a killer? A multiple murderer? It wasn't possible. Was it? I watched my untouched cup on the table swing back and forth.

"I don't believe it. Karen wouldn't kill anyone."

"Maybe not," Montero said, "but we need to talk with her to find that out."

"Rachel, if you have any idea where she might be, we need to know it."

"Frank, I don't know where she is. I wish I did."

Standish poured more coffee for everyone. I hoped he turned off the coffee maker.

"I think she's hiding her. That's why Tanaka came back. To be with her lover. I think that's who was here the other night."

"It wasn't Karen. You're pissing me off, Marty, but if you think you *really* need to know, I'll give you her name and number."

Frank passed me his notepad and pen. So much for trust, Papa Bear.

"If you haven't seen or spoken to Tanaka in a year, how did you know she was in Florida?" Lockhart asked.

"I'm a detective."

Montero tapped the warrant lying on the table. "Is there anything here that was hers? That could help us find her?"

I took them into Karen's studio and opened the closet. "That's everything of hers."

Standish was looking at the paintings on the walls. He checked behind them to see if anything was hidden there, started to take one off the wall.

"The paintings are mine."

"The signature says K. Tanaka."

"They were gifts."

"Let it go, Marty." Frank said. "Give us a hand here."

They pulled out a dozen boxes and Karen's computer. They left the drawing table and easels. They opened each box even though I had carefully listed the contents on the top. I hated watching them go through her things. Montero took me aside.

"Why don't you show me the other rooms?"

We went through the guest bath and third bedroom, the living room/dining area, Karen's unused office that had been the dining room, the kitchen, laundry alcove, my bedroom and bath.

"This place is bigger than my house. Being a PI must pay

pretty well."

"Not really. I bought when the market was soft on a GI loan. Karen helped with payments. It's tight since she left, but I manage."

Why was I saying so much?

"By the way, the extradition on Jerry Harris finally came through. We pick him up next week, and Barrow's back in jail."

"Glad to hear it. Did he lose his bond?"

"New charges were filed; he's still got connections so he'll be out by tonight most likely. Also, at the end of May someone sent me a bottle of Balvenie with a note saying 'to sweeten your coffee.' Wasn't you, was it?"

"Why would I do that?"

"Can't say. Just wanted to thank whoever sent it; it is a nice sweetener."

I didn't let Montero's friendly patter or sad looks fool me. While Frank is a warm cuddly chocolate grizzly bear, Montero is a rumpled bloodhound with long, saggy features. He makes it look casual but he's thorough and doesn't miss much. He pulled out every drawer, opened every door; looked behind, under and in everything. It made me angry to see him rustling through my underwear. I suddenly realized how Louise felt about my going through her husband's things.

Montero took two large framed photographs from my closet and propped them against a wall. They were black-and-white photos of a nude woman (me) lying amongst driftwood by the river in early morning light, mist rising from the water. He knelt down to study them.

"I think I know that spot. My son and I go fishing there all the time. Why don't you hang these?"

"Haven't decided where yet."

"They're very good. You should put them up. Did Tanaka take these?"

"No. They're by a local photographer. They're part of a series he's doing."

"What's his name? I'd like to see more of his work."

Montero—an art lover? "Roger Burke. He's in the phone book."

"Thanks. My wife and I collect photography: Ansel Adams, Annie Liebowitz, Margret Burke-White, Albert Watson and several others. We have a *Nuba* by Leni Riefenstahl. I think we'd like to add this guy. Not a picture of you, of course; too many people would talk. But these are good. You really should hang them."

I knew that Frank and Lorraine collected primitive African masks, but I hadn't thought of cops being art collectors.

Montero stood up. "I know you don't want to think that your friend is a killer. But look at the evidence. Two identified victims in different cities where she's lived who look just like her. A third victim who I'm willing to bet will look like her too. All disposed of in a similar manner. Her being seen with Nagasawa's car."

"You don't know that was Karen. Maybe it's another look-alike."

"Following her from city to city? Do you really believe that?"

"But it's possible. Why would Karen kill these women?"

"I don't know. Because she hates herself, but is afraid of suicide? Because she wants to be unique? I'll let the psychiatrists and profilers figure that out. I just need to find her."

Lockhart came into the room. "We have what we need."

"Okay. Then we'll be leaving. I'm sorry for what you're going through, but it can't be helped. I've got this gut feeling that there are other victims out there, waiting to be found. I don't want it to happen again. If you see or hear from your friend, call us."

They left with two boxes of Karen's personal items, mostly old papers, and her computer and discs. Lockhart gave me a receipt. The other boxes they left on the studio floor without putting anything back into them. I sat on the floor and began repacking, looked around at Karen's paintings: at the *Madonna*, at the one of me.

"Stay still. Look at me. Eyes nearly closed. That's it. That's the tilt I want. Now stay still."

Karen worked steadily, her dark eyes darting from me to the canvas, her brushstrokes sure and fluid, laying the paint on thickly, wet-on-wet, mixing color directly on the canvas. The room was warm enough for me to be comfortably naked leaning against the cushioned board, my left hand tucked behind my back, the right behind my head. Karen, naked to the waist, wore only paint-spattered jeans; her small taut breasts barely jiggled as she worked, pink nipples erect. She glowed from her efforts. Her long black hair was piled high to stay out of the way. One errant strand hung beautifully down.

"Stop smiling. Stay still."

Something wet touched my nipple. I opened my eyes. Karen, smiling, dabbed my nose with the wet brush.

"Fall asleep? We're done for today." She twirled the brush in her hand. "Only water." She leaned in, kissed me, melded her body to mine.

The painting of me hung where I had posed; where Karen and I made love that day; where Wendy and I . . . I picked up a kimono that had belonged to Karen's grandmother, held it to my face and cried.

Sixteen

It was after two before I made it into the office. Both Doris and Mary were at the reception desk.

"We're sorry, Rachel." Doris handed me another search warrant and a receipt. "We didn't have a choice."

"That cocky bastard actually came back with a warrant," Mary said.

"What did he take?"

"Just a folder of papers off one of your tables."

"He didn't go in the closet?"

"No. It was locked and we don't have a key. He called someone to ask if he should break it down. Then he just left with the stuff on the table."

"Okay. Thanks."

Doris handed me a folder. "This was waiting in the fax machine this morning. We didn't tell him about it. The warrant only said he could search *your* office, not ours."

"Thanks again."

Things in my office were neat but not exactly as I left them. I probably had Doris or Mary to thank for that. I felt sure that Standish left things scattered and all of the doors and drawers opened. My entire file on Karen was gone from table two. At least he didn't take my computer where I kept back-up files. Also, my original field notes were locked in the closet. Still, it irritated me.

The folder Doris gave me held a fax from Helen. I called her. She wasn't in her office, but I reached her at home.

"I thought you'd be working. Are you starting the holiday early?"

"Hardly. I expect to be working all weekend. I'm taking a break to get windows boarded up before Frances gets here."

"How bad is it?"

"Terrible. They cancelled tomorrow's Gator game. Otherwise, okay so far. She's not expected to hit land until tomorrow afternoon. She's fat and slow, but she's going to dump all over this state before she quits singing. Did you get my fax?"

"Yes, thank you."

"I left a message for you last night, but I didn't get the DMV trace back on the car until this morning. And you were right; there was a request from your police department. I sent them the same info."

"I know. They visited me this morning. According to your fax, Karen took off the morning after you saw her in November."

"That's right. I spoke with some neighbors and the landlord. She was a quiet renter. No one really knew her, except to say 'Hi' or wave. Then she suddenly left. The car trace said she sold the car the same day in Jacksonville. I spoke with the dealer. He said he remembered she was in a hurry and that she'd take less than wholesale for a cash sale. She had the title and Florida ID, so he jumped on it. She told him she was going home to San Diego. A taxi took her to the airport. She had no reservation, and she didn't fly out under her own name, if that's really where she went. I've made a request for information on the taxi and from the airlines based on the police inquiry, but I don't expect answers soon, if at all. This happened nearly ten months ago."

"What happened with her things she left behind?"

"Landlord sold them. He didn't know she had cut out until mid-December when he went looking for the late rent. He had the utilities shut off and put her stuff in storage. Everything was auctioned off in February for back payment. I'm sorry that things are turning out this way for you."

"Thanks."

"I hope you realize I can't do any more personal favors with this. It's an official investigation now. My follow-ups are on company time and equipment. What you've got is all you get."

"I know that. And I really appreciate everything you've done. Thanks, Helen. My best wishes to you and your family. I hope that hurricane goes a different way."

"Me too. Bye."

So, Karen, what kind of hurricane are you? I put the fax down and went to the blackboard. I wrote "Karen" large in the middle of the board. To the left, I put "San Mateo—born 1973. BA/MFA UC Berkeley—'97." Beneath that, "Evelyn Martinez—disappeared (murdered?) '98/body found 2000." To the right, "Gainesville—Sep-Nov '03." I drew a long arrow sweeping around to the lower left and wrote "San Diego/home?"

Tori lives in Ramona, California, but she said she hadn't heard from Karen. Was she lying? Is Ramona near San Diego? Was there other family in that area? Her parents still live in San Mateo. I added all that to the board. Beneath Karen's name I put "Aug 28: seen at river and Westbrook Mall. Aiko Nagasawa—murdered. Unknown—murdered '02? Both found at river site. Others????"

God, I hoped not.

I stepped back. It didn't tell me much. Beneath Karen's name, I wrote "Met—Mar '98/moved in together Sep 2000/left Sep '03. Why?" As I recalled it, I added "Started Cramer College—Jan '98." I looked over at my note on Martinez's disappearance. I added "Date of disappearance?" and circled it. Maybe Martinez was still alive when Karen came here. I hoped so. Beneath Gainesville I wrote Helen's comment, "Cold? Aloof? Nervous?" I underlined each word. I inserted "Look-alike" at "seen at river."

I drew a large heart around Karen's name and wrote "Sweet. Loving. Caring. Imp!!!"

The room felt cold. I checked the thermostat. It was set at 78 degrees. It felt colder. Maybe I felt colder. Outside it was in the high eighties. Clouds hid the sun at the moment but there was a lot of blue sky. I slumped on the loveseat.

Four women: Karen, Aiko, Evelyn and someone else. I pictured their faces. So alike, yet distinctly different. I made up a face for the unknown woman, a blend of the other three. Together, you could tell them apart. If you knew one of them, no problem, the others would be different. But if you didn't know them and saw one of them one place and another somewhere else, would you think you saw the same woman?

I didn't want to give Montero's theory any credence, but it was hard. I loved Karen and couldn't believe her capable of murder. Was Evelyn killed when they both lived in San Mateo? Did they know each other? The unknown woman died while Karen and I lived together. Had Karen known her? From where? Wouldn't I know if I were living with a murderer? Had Gacy's wife known?

The woman in the security photo looked an awful lot like Karen. But it couldn't be. Could it? Were there other bodies out there waiting to be found? Is that why Karen suddenly ran away? If it is, why did she come back? Where was she now?

I went back to the blackboard. The security photo was taken at 7:45 AM. The mall wouldn't be open that early. She just dumped the car there. Where did she go? How did she leave the area? I drew an arrow from "Westbrook Mall" and wrote "Destination?" I put a circle around it.

My office phone rang.

"It's Rod. We have a problem."

"What?"

"When you were at Stanley's, did you take any of the

videotapes with you?"

I thought of the copy I made of Jackie and Dorian.

"No. I left everything as I found it. There was a tape in the VCR and two untitled cassettes on the shelves that contained the personal porn. Just like I told you."

"They're gone. Carson called a few minutes ago. He and Jablowski are there with sheriff's deputies checking the place out. Apparently someone broke a window to get into the house. He said the place was neat as a pin but that the tapes were missing along with all of the commercial porn and maybe a John Wayne and a James Bond film."

"Which ones?"

"How would I know? And why those? The place is now a crime scene."

"Is Amber okay?"

"Who's Amber?"

"The cat. She's an orange tabby. I left food and water for her."

"I don't know. Who do you think broke in? Could it have been your client?"

"Carter? I doubt it. He has his own keys."

"Aren't those the ones you gave us?"

"Right."

"Who else knew about the tapes?"

"Gordon the pizza boy and Cameron from the shoe store. I told both of them that you would probably be looking at them. I would think that everyone who was on them would know about them. The two guys at the Manhole said they knew that Stanley liked to take pictures. If Stanley was abducted, maybe it was whoever has him."

"Wouldn't they have his keys?"

"I guess. I don't know what to think."

"That Gordon kid? He also works at the convenience store, right?"

"Yes."

"Okay. I'll have Carson and Jablowski swing by and

interview him and then the shoe guy again. You said they weren't too keen on those tapes being seen."

"No, they weren't. One of them could have broken in. Any leads on Stanley yet?"

"No. Talk to you later."

I wandered about the office. Looked at the blackboard. It wasn't giving me any answers. I made out an index card for the Stanley file: "Who stole the tapes? Gordon? Cameron? Carter? Which John Wayne tape? Which Bond? Why take those?" I had the tape I made. Maybe it was time to check that out. I turned on my computer and did a property search of the address Gordon gave me for Jackie and Dorian. I wanted to know more about them.

The owners were Doctors Dorian W. and Jacqueline Losey. Did the W stand for Wayne? Just what I needed. I googled their names and did a Lexis-Nexis. Dr. Jackie was a psychology professor at Cramer College. Had she known Karen? Wrong case, but who knows? It might be worth a shot. Dr. Dorian was a gynecologist with his own practice. They were in their late fifties. They had a triple-A credit rating. Neither had ever been arrested. Dr. Dorian was sued twice for malpractice but was exonerated both times. I called their home but no answer. I'd try again later.

A lot of my work is at the computer—there's so much information out there. It's a real time saver at times, but now it wasn't telling me what I really wanted to know: where was Stanley? Where was Karen?

To work off some of the frustration, I updated my files on Carter and Stanley and wrote the final report for Louise. Then I rebuilt the folder on Karen. It wasn't enough; I needed to be out—doing something, anything.

Seventeen

FRANK HAD SAID BEYOND North Ferry just inside the city and by the river. That's a lot of territory, and many small dirt roads lead to the river. Roads people use to go fishing or hiking or picnicking or disposing of unwanted trash.

The road I wanted turned out to be easy to find. A barricade and a patrol car blocked it. I kept going. A hundred yards further was the city limits sign and River Drive became County Road 1 again. I turned down the first road I came to beyond the city line. It was well used, rutted and dusty. I drove slowly and could see where others had pulled off and dumped various things they didn't want to pay to take to the county landfill. The road led to the river and a natural launch site.

A white Ford pick-up with boat trailer attached was parked off to the side. The boat was gone, and I didn't see anyone. I parked out of the way. I exchanged my pumps for a pair of walkers, doused myself with bug spray. A path led me along the riverbank south.

The path twisted around shrubbery and thickets, moving away and then back closer to the river. It was hot and muggy with no breeze whenever I moved away from the water. There were many places where people stopped to fish, and I relished each time the path brought me to one. The slight winds off the water dried the sweat and helped cool me. I should have brought something to drink. There were few large trees; it was mostly scrub that picked at my jacket and pants, pulling threads. As I walked, I tried to listen for voices. I didn't want to walk straight into an active search.

It was slow going. I needed to walk about a third of a mile, maybe 600 yards, but it seemed to take forever in the oppressive air. I barely noticed how far I had come until I walked into the yellow police tape stretched across the path. The tape went off both to my left and right through the scrub. I pitied whoever had had to secure the area. I ducked under the tape and kept walking.

The path led back to the river. There the tape stretched along the bank for several hundred feet. Beached ahead of me was a small boat with an outboard motor. In the boat were rods and tackle, empty soda cans and an ice chest; but no fish, and no fisherman. Maybe he stopped off to use the bushes. Or maybe, like me, he was curious. In the chest were ice, melted water and five cans of soda. In this heat they were tempting, but I don't do Dr. Pepper, diet or otherwise. I took a couple pieces of ice and sucked on them.

I heard voices. I moved back down the path and into the bushes. Two men appeared. They wore baseball caps and fishing vests, but one was carrying a black bag and had a camera around his neck. I stepped back onto the path and walked toward them.

"Hi, Andy. Clyde. How's the fishing?"

Andy Walther and Clyde Normand work for the *Daily Record*, the city's major newspaper. Clyde, one of the paper's photographers, is in his mid-fifties. Andy's a reporter. He does tear-your-heart-out features or exposés; they're all the same to him. I don't generally like reporters, but Andy's more human than most. We met when I investigated to see if he was cheating on his wife. He wasn't. Since then we'd become professional friends and trade occasional information. When I forced Deputy Mayor Barrow's confession to the killings and harassment at the Kathouse and other crimes, I gave one of the recordings I made to Andy. This was the first time I'd ever seen him without his tweed jacket and knit tie.

"Not bad," Andy said. "Haven't seen you in a couple months. Out for a walk?"

"Have to keep my girlish figure. Catch anything interesting?"

"Andy," Clyde said, "we better get back."

"Just a second. Why are you out here, Rachel?"

"Probably the same reason you are."

Andy thought for a moment. "Where are you parked?"

"Back a ways. Is that your white pick-up and trailer?"

"It's Clyde's. Clyde, why don't you go back to the office? I'll stay with Rachel. Pass me a couple sodas. You want one, Rachel?"

"No thanks."

We watched as Clyde pushed off, started the motor, and headed upstream. Andy opened one of the sodas and drank it down in one long pull. I shuddered. He offered the other again, but I shook my head. No how. No way. He put it in a vest pocket. He crushed the empty and put that in a pocket too.

"What's your interest, Rachel?"

"The victims and the woman the police are looking for resemble a friend of a client." I'm the client. "I'm trying to figure out if she's involved in any way."

"Who is she? Do the police know about her?"

"I can't say at this point. Too many questions and not enough answers."

"You think looking at where the bodies were found will help?"

"Maybe."

"Come on. I'll give you the tour."

Andy took me along another path through the thicket. We came to an open area that acted as a turnaround and car park. There was a clear view of the river, but no place to launch a boat—except maybe a canoe. The dirt road twisted away westward. The city had provided a trash barrel to lessen littering. It was empty, and the area was clean of trash. Probably picked up by the police looking for possible evidence. I didn't envy whoever had to go through that stuff. I hoped it was Standish. Andy and I walked to a large hole in the ground that was surrounded by police tape. It was out of the main parking area set back from the edge of the road; over time cars pulling in and out had created a private parking lane.

The hole was at least 10 feet long, 8 feet wide and about 5 feet deep. It seemed too large for disposing of a body. It would have taken hours to dig.

"Is this where they found Nagasawa?"

"Yes. And the other body too. If you look over there," Andy pointed to the river, "that's where the fisherman was when he saw the woman burying Nagasawa's body here."

"And the other body was already buried here?"

"Pretty close. As I understand it, Nagasawa was lying in the hole about here." Andy pointed to an area close to us. "She was curled in a fetal position inside a trash bag. The car was backed up to the hole with the trunk open. The body was half-buried when the fisherman scared the woman off. The other body was found a little more to the right yesterday."

"How did they find her?"

"A guy walking his dog. Apparently when they removed Nagasawa's body, they made the hole larger but hadn't filled it in. It rained heavily over the weekend and more dirt must have been washed down. Anyway, yesterday Gregory Dotson is out here with his Great Dane, Brutus. The dog jumps in the hole and starts digging. Gregory is worried they'll get in trouble because of the crime scene tape. So he's calling to the dog, but Brutus keeps digging away. Won't listen. Then the dog finds a trash bag and is clawing at it and comes up out of the hole with a bone in his mouth. It was either a leg or arm bone. Gregory is now sure that they are in trouble, but he does the right thing, anyway, and calls the police. The police recovered the second body, then expanded the hole until they were sure they were digging in virgin soil."

Andy moved away from the hole to the edge of the road and pointed.

"You can see more crime tape down there. The police question is: if you find a second body in the same manner, might there be a third? Or more? So they brought a cadaver dog out to search the area. They've gotten two hits so far, but both turned out to be animal carcasses. They're coming out again tomorrow."

I stepped into the road. The afternoon sun was bright, and I shaded my eyes. I could see the police tape Andy had pointed to about 50 yards away. This wasn't good. Please, don't let there be more bodies.

"Andy," my throat was dry. I couldn't speak. I pictured Aiko Nagasawa, Evelyn Martinez and the unknown woman. I saw them standing, smiling, alive. I saw them curled up, stuffed into black trash bags, buried in lonely unknown places. Three look-a-likes. Three. I was never great at math, but I know that it takes three to make a series. A series of similar murders means a serial killer. I saw shadowy figures, victims, fading into the distance. I pictured Karen and the woman in the security photograph. I merged their images; then split them again. Which are you, Karen? Which are you?

I vaguely heard the pop of a soda can top. I felt the cool cylinder pressed into my hand. I automatically raised it to my mouth. I swallowed several gulps before the taste registered.

"God, Andy! Are you trying to poison me? Yuck."

I handed him back the can. He laughed.

"It's not that bad," he said, finishing it.

"I ought to make you walk home, or bury you here."

My thoughtless comment made me shiver.

"Are you all right?"

"Yeah. I just had what Yogi called déjà vu all over again. I remembered all the bodies found at Tierney's place. This reminds me of that."

"Speaking of which, when are we going to write that book?"

"What book?"

"*The Confessions of Madame Gumshoe.*"

"By Rachel Cord, PI, as told to Andy Walther."

"That's the one. You still owe me that interview of what really happened."

I shivered again. "Not yet."

There wasn't anything else to say. We headed back the way we had come. Andy crushed the can and put it in a pocket. At least he didn't litter. We didn't speak until I let him off at the *Daily Record* building downtown.

"You know I'm going to find out who your client's friend is. Why don't you just tell me?"

"Go earn your money, Andy. I'm still trying to sort things out. I'll talk with you later."

I went home and threw my ruined jacket and pants in the trash. I went into the shower, let the hot water blister me as I turned in slow circles, willing it to purge me of demons: Karen running from me; Karen pushing a heavy trash bag into a hole; Wendy's warm body against mine on the cool linoleum; Danny biting me; Wendy walking away, closing a door; Danny's sad smile; Karen's face multiplied two, four, eight, 16 times.

Wrapped in my white terry robe, sipping Glenfiddich, I called Wendy. Clare answered.

"Wendy still doesn't want to speak with you. I'm sorry."

"Would you tell her two things for me, please? Tell her, people make mistakes. Tell her that . . ." I think I love her. "That I'd like a second chance."

"Is THERE A COOKIE CUTTER killer on the loose? Good evening, I'm Sandra Young."

"And I'm Gary Bentley. It would seem that way as police

investigate what appears to be a series of look-alike deaths. Tanya Waverly has our report."

I lay curled on my sofa still wearing my robe; the mushu pork and fried dumplings I had ordered, and my glass of Glenfiddich, barely touched. Channel 3's *Late Night Report* was just starting.

Tanya Waverly (*on camera*): "It's quiet here on the edge of the city. At this time of night only late night fishermen or amorous teens looking for somewhere to park would normally use the dirt road behind me. But not tonight. Tonight, police block this road because down that dark lane someone has been burying bodies.

"Early last Saturday morning, Raymond Beaudreau was here hoping to catch fish; he caught something else instead."

Beaudreau (*file footage of earlier interview*): "I come up the bank and thought I saw a woman burying trash. That's illegal. This ain't a dump, so I yelled at her. She drove off real quick. Then I saw that what she was burying was a body. I called the police as soon as I could."

(*Scene changes to daytime footage of medical examiner's van coming down dirt road and entering onto highway.*)

Waverly's voice: "Police soon arrived and recovered the body of Aiko Nagasawa (*portrait of Nagasawa*), a local jeweler and businesswoman, wrapped in garbage bags. Her car, the one Beaudreau saw driving away, was later found abandoned at Westbrook Mall. Then yesterday afternoon, things got worse. Gregory Dotson and his dog, Brutus, were out walking in this area and found another buried body.

Dotson (*file footage of Dotson and dog*): "Scared the heck out of me. Brutus was rooting around where they had that police tape up, and I'm yelling at him to come here, when he brings back a femur or something. I called Nine-One-One on my cell right away."

Waverly (*on camera*): "According to our sources, the second body was found practically where Nagasawa was buried and was also wrapped in garbage bags. As yet the body has not been identified, but we are told that it is an Asian-American woman in her late twenties or early thirties. Then this morning, local authorities investigating leads were notified of a similar case in San Mateo, California.

"In December 1997, Evelyn Martinez *(portrait of Martinez)*, an Hispanic-Japanese-American, disappeared from her home in San Mateo. Her body was found two years later buried in a rural area wrapped in garbage bags.

"Currently, local authorities are trying to find this woman, *(portrait of Karen from Cramer College yearbook)* Karen Tanaka, a former professor at Cramer College who they say may or may not be involved in these killings. Tanaka lived in San Mateo before arriving here in 1998. I'm Tanya Waverly for Channel Three TV News."

Young *(on camera with Bentley)*: "Thank you, Tanya. If anyone has any information about these women and events, or knows the whereabouts of Karen Tanaka, they are urged to call the police or 'Crime Stop' at Five-Four-Three-S-T-O-P. 'Crime Stop' informants may remain anonymous and are eligible for rewards."

Eighteen

I HADN'T GOTTEN DRUNK and, for a change, I hadn't waited up and called Margo. I used him too often to fill losses and gaps in my life instead of for the sheer enjoyment his voice brings me. That *Voice* is like a great Scotch and I had been wasting both lately. It was a bad night and I had no idea how I was going to make things right with Wendy. I was wasting her too.

At 7:15 AM, I was in the east parking lot at Westbrook Mall sipping coffee and studying the security camera photo I cut from the newspaper. I had pasted it to one side of a five-by-eight index card. The newspaper photo of Aiko Nagasawa and one of Karen I pasted on the other side.

Westbrook Mall was one of those monster labyrinths with limited access surrounded by parking lots. On Saturdays it opens at nine. There were large banners promoting Labor Day Weekend sales. Aiko Nagasawa's killer abandoned Aiko's car somewhere in this lot the previous Saturday. Exactly where didn't matter. I was trying to figure where the woman went afterward. What her plan was.

The picture was taken from high up and showed the woman walking at an angle from left to right across a parking lot. The sun was off to her left rear so she was mostly in shadow.

I got out of my car and walked toward the south end of the massive building. High on the wall at the corner were two security cameras. One pointed northeast the other southwest. I compared the camera angles to the picture and where I would have to stand to match the photo. The northeast camera took this picture I was pretty sure. Did the police have the tape from the other camera? Did it show where the woman went?

There were service entrances to the mall at the corner. Did the woman work here? Was she that stupid? A lot of people who commit crimes are, and they always seem so surprised when they get caught. But the police would have checked the mall thoroughly, and the woman was still free. Ergo, she didn't work here and wasn't that stupid. Far across the south parking lot was a city bus stop. I walked over to check the schedules.

The bus stop was a large covered island on a frontage road near the edge of the parking lot where buses could approach from both directions. Six buses, Monday through Saturday, arrived and departed starting at 7:45 AM; two more came at 8:00 and another six at 8:15. This routine continued until 10:00 PM. The time stamp on the photo Standish showed me had read 0745. If one of the buses was running late she might have caught it, or she had to wait until 8:00. That's if the security camera's clock was accurate and if she took a bus. I couldn't see the woman waiting around any longer.

Aiko Nagasawa was a local jeweler. Did she have a store or kiosk in this mall? Is this where her killer first saw her? Why was she killed? Why were any of them killed? Martinez or that other woman who was just found? Has she been identified yet? What did they have in common besides looking like Karen? Was that why they were killed? It seemed such a stupid reason. How would any of them and Karen have met?

At 7:34, two middle-aged Hispanic women in uniforms with large canvas shopping bags were the first riders to arrive.

Probably housekeepers on their way to work.

"Excuse me, please. Can you help me? I'm an investigator."

I held out my SAPI card. Both seemed suddenly wary and one gripped the other's arm tightly. I held up the photos of Aiko and Karen.

"Were you here last Saturday? Did you see someone who looked like this get on a bus? She would have been wearing dark jeans, a sweatshirt and a baseball cap."

The woman doing the gripping spoke rapidly in Spanish in the other woman's ear. She looked scared. The only word I understood was "immigración."

"No. No." I shook my head and smiled. "I'm not with Immigration. No immigración. Please. I'm a private detective. I'm looking for a woman who looks like this."

"You are not Immigration?" The other woman asked.

"No, please. I'm just trying to find someone. She may have been here last Saturday about this time waiting for a bus."

"We didn't see her. We can't help you."

They moved to the end of the island and kept watching me. The woman who spoke with me kept trying to calm the other one.

Other riders arrived: a hospital worker, a carpenter with tool belt, a grandmotherly type and some retail workers. None had seen the woman I wanted.

A car pulled up at the nearest parking spaces, and the man and woman in it sat there talking. I walked over to the driver's side. The woman lowered the window part way when I showed my card. I asked my questions and showed them the pictures.

"We saw these pictures in the paper this morning," the woman said. She indicated Aiko Nagasawa. "Isn't she dead? And this other woman, aren't the police looking for her? Was she here?"

"Someone who looks like her. Right about this time last

Saturday."

"Sorry. We didn't see her."

"Do you know if the buses were all on time last Saturday."

"I think so. My husband's anyway. Several arrived at the same time."

Buses started arriving. I spoke with each of the drivers. The police had asked all of them the same questions. None had seen the woman. When the buses left, I was alone.

If she didn't get on a bus, where did she go? Beyond the frontage road was North Ferry Avenue, the main east/west street on the north side of the city. Beyond it was a strip mall with grocery store, some retail businesses and fast food restaurants. There were apartment complexes and residential areas. It seemed endless. I looked back at Westbrook Mall. Would she have been able to go in the service entrances? Would there be a security camera inside? The police probably checked that.

As I waited for the eight o'clock buses, an old man shuffled to the bus stop and sat. He wore khaki pants, a short-sleeved flowered shirt and a baseball cap. His brown leather shoes were polished. Under his arm, he carried a paper grocery bag with the top rolled closed. I showed him the pictures.

"Pretty woman," he said. "Looks a lot like my wife did. Sat right over there."

He pointed to the end of the island. My heart skipped a beat. His watery blue eyes went unfocused as he seemed to recall something; he had a wistful smile.

He refocused on me. "Why are you looking for her?"

"The police are looking for her too. She's connected to a murder investigation. These pictures have been in the news."

"Don't watch the news or read the paper anymore. It's always the same: something bad happening. Don't need it. Don't want it."

He looked at the pictures again and sighed. "Something

bad always happens."

He handed back the pictures, opened his paper bag and took out a half slice of toasted bread, then rolled the top closed again. He broke pieces off and fed them to some sparrows that were searching the gutter.

"Did you see if she got on a bus?"

"Who?"

"This woman." I showed him the security picture again. "You said she sat over there."

"Pretty woman. Looks like my wife. Slim, boyish figure. Long, black hair in a ponytail." He sighed again. "Did I tell you about my wife? We met in '46 in Japan. That was 'Occupied Japan' then. I was in the Army, barely eighteen. Lied about my age in '44 to get in the war. Wanted to kill Japs." He shook his head as he watched the birds. "What did I know? Wonderful woman. Married fifty-three years. Died in her sleep. Rolled over to kiss her one morning, but she was gone."

He tossed more bread to the sparrows.

"Did this woman get on a bus?"

He nodded and smiled. "Eastbound Loop. Same as me. I was hoping she would. Wasn't sure that she would though. She kept waiting like she wanted the Westbound. The Westbound is always late on Saturdays; don't know why. She got on at the last moment. Sat in the back. Hid under her cap. It was a Cardinals cap. Pretty woman. Did I tell you she looks like my wife? It wasn't easy having a Japanese wife right after the war. Lots of prejudice. But we were in love. Married fifty-three years. Went to kiss her, but she wasn't there anymore."

"Do you remember where this woman got off the bus? Did she get off before you did?"

He nodded. "Riverside Park. Same as me. Right by Sam's Deli. Do you know Sam's Deli? Every Saturday I get off there and walk in the park to feed the birds. Sam's isn't open on Saturday though. Sam was in the war. Europe. Made great pastrami sandwiches. But not on Saturdays. His son runs the deli now. Sandwiches just as good as his dad's. You ever been there? Great place. They got a wall covered with pictures of people in the war. Other wars too. Keiko and I are there. Our wedding picture. Me in uniform; her in a kimono. You should go there sometime. Great sandwiches. But Sam's gone now. Soon we'll all be gone. Fifty-three years."

"May I drive you to the park? Could you show me where this woman went?"

It was a slow walk to my car then we drove to Riverside Park. His name was Paul Jensen. He didn't talk much about his World War II experiences, but he told me about Keiko, how they met and came back to the States and their 53 years together. How they raised five daughters, all married now, and about his 17 grandchildren and four great grandchildren.

This early, it was easy to find parking at Riverside Park. Later in the day it would be full of people. The park is a mile plus swath of green space overlooking the river along River Drive.

I reminded Mr. Jensen of the woman on the bus. "Did you see where she went after you got off the bus?"

"We got off right over there." He pointed to the bus stop next to Sam's Deli & Catering. "She got out at the back. I went out the front because I sit right behind the driver. Had to wait for traffic before crossing the street. I wanted to speak to her, tell her how much she looks like my wife, but I didn't want her getting the wrong idea from an old man. Pretty woman." (sigh) "Married fifty-three years. Wanted to kiss her, but she was gone."

"Which way did the she go?"

"My wife? Oh, the woman. Probably think I'm senile, don't you? But she looks so much like my wife. Nearly five years now, but I still miss her every day."

He got that faraway look again, then turned and pointed south.

"She went down to the restrooms over there. Got a drink of water and stood around for several minutes. Then she was gone. Didn't see her again. Must have looked away to feed the birds or something." He shook his paper bag.

"Thank you, Mr. Jensen. You've been a lot of help."

The public restroom was a plain brown cinder block building, MEN to the left, WOMEN to the right, and a drinking fountain in the center. Why did the woman stand here for several minutes? What was she thinking, deciding? Where was she going? Was someone meeting her? Was she really Karen? My condo was only a 16-block walk from here. We had walked it many times. If it was Karen, why didn't she come to me? Why didn't she stay on the bus at least until it turned onto Cutter Avenue? It would have been a shorter walk.

I could understand Karen coming to a familiar place, to an area she knew well. But what about the woman in the photo who had killed Aiko and dumped the car at Westbrook Mall? Was this her destination? Did she live near here? Jensen thought she really wanted the West Loop bus. Then why get off here? Why not stay on the East Loop until it changed around to the West and dropped you where you really wanted to be? Or, if this were her destination, why wait to get on the bus?

I had no answers and no clues to pursue. I looked over to Sam's Deli. Too bad they weren't open. I could use one of their great bagels and coffee. The wall Jensen spoke of is covered in photos of soldiers, sailors, airmen and Marines from World War II to the present. Customers keep bringing in pictures, and Reuben and Esther Feinstein add them to the wall that included family pictures of Sam, Reuben, and a Saul now stationed in Iraq. My grandfather's WWII picture is there as well as one of my brother, Wally, graduating from West Point, and one of me with "Hot Rod" Rodecker and Helen Abernathy.

I wish Sam's had been open on Saturdays; then that woman may have gone in and ordered something, and I'd have a clue as to where she was and who she was. But if wishes were horses, we'd . . . Hell, I was up to my neck in horseshit already; I didn't need any more.

Just north of Sam's was the Bluffs at Riverside, a luxury townhouse project. Construction was continuing. A new sign read, "70% sold! Prime views still available."

Back in May, someone had been harassing and beating people from Miss Kitty's Kathouse Kabaret two blocks south. I had been hired to find out the who and why of the harassment. I found out, but not soon enough. It turned out to be workers from the Bluffs site who were working for the ex-deputy mayor to put the Kathouse out of business. The two blocks that included the Kathouse and Sam's Deli were wanted for a Phase II of the Riverside project. Vincent Barrow owned half of the properties and stood to make a lot of money on the deal. The Kathouse was the only holdout. The harassment escalated; three people died, including Dominick "El Gallo" Guerrero, construction foreman at the Bluffs and leader of the harassers, who was shot by Barrow for wanting out of the scheme.

These were painful memories. Sarah Hastings died on the sidewalk outside of the Kathouse. I helped catch the bastards responsible, but that didn't lessen her loss or my feelings of inadequacy.

Now I struck out again. I lost Sarah before we even had a chance at a beginning, and I was chasing the ghost of Karen. What about Wendy? Would she, could she, forgive me? Give me another chance?

I watched Paul Jensen feed the birds and thought about him and Keiko married 53 years. He started out hating the Japanese and ended married to a Japanese woman. Maybe Wendy would take me back. I certainly hoped so. I took out my cell phone and turned it on. Checked to see if possibly she had left a message. Not. I put the phone back in my pocket.

I walked south toward the Kathouse. The second-hand furniture store, Riverside Furnishings, was open and having a going-out-of-business sale. I went in. A man and woman were moving a sofa to a new location. About a third of the display area was empty.

"Make us an offer on anything you want," the man said. "Buy three items, and we'll take an extra ten percent off the final sale."

"Buy five," the woman offered, "and we'll give you a sixth free."

"Sounds like a bargain, but I need information, not furniture. Were you open last Saturday at this time? Did you see one of these women or someone who looks like them?"

They looked at the photos of Karen and Nagasawa and shook their heads "no."

"She had long, black hair in a ponytail and would have been wearing dark jeans, a sweatshirt, and a Cardinals baseball hat."

The woman shook her head again. "Sorry. Can't help you. Sure you don't need some furniture?"

"No, thanks."

The auto parts store was closed permanently with a sign giving their new location. Secure Moving & Storage was open but no help. At the Kathouse, I stood by the lamppost where Sarah had hit her head and died, knelt and touched the curb where her blood had flowed into the gutter.

My phone rang. It was Wendy. I took a deep breath and answered it.

"Hi."

"Mother said I should hear you out. I'm listening."

I sat on the curb leaning against the lamppost. Where to start? What to say?

Say something! This isn't Margo, for god's sake, who'll listen to your silent crap.

"Wendy . . . I . . . Wendy, I'm sorry. I know that's not enough to say. What I did was wrong. I didn't want to tell you because I knew it would hurt you. But I had to tell you because hiding it was a bigger wrong. I . . ."

The words came out in spurts surrounded by silence. I

told her everything about Danny—both times—knowing it would hurt, but having to be honest. I talked about finding Carter and my flashbacks; about being scared that Karen was a murderer; about the police searching my home and office; about every moment since leaving her Wednesday morning. She didn't respond, but didn't hang up, either. I talked and rambled, repeating myself, mixing things up just as they were mixed in my head—even including my obsession with Margo—and not always sure what I had said or not said. But interwoven into my ramblings I kept telling her, "I love you," and knew it was true.

"Wendy, I hope you can forgive me; that you'll give me another chance. If not, I want to at least stay your friend."

"Rachel, I don't want you as a friend."

Her words stabbed me. Tears welled in my eyes; my throat tightened; I couldn't breathe or swallow.

"I wanted you to be my love; wanted to be yours. We made no promises, true, hadn't spoken, but . . . Maybe I wanted it too badly, too soon, and that's why your confession hurt so much; felt like such a betrayal. I wanted it all, Rachel. All or nothing."

I began to breathe again. "Wendy—"

"We can have brunch tomorrow at South Ferry Transportation; departure is eleven o'clock. Let's see what happens after that."

I was shaking. Shaking with relief, shaking with hope, shaking with fear. I could still lose Wendy, but she was giving us a shot. I got up and took a deep breath, pulled tissues from my bag to dry my face, looked up at the beautiful blue sky. Then I saw the security cameras on the corner of the building.

Nineteen

I SPEED-DIALED MARGO.

It rang six times before he picked up. *"Ooooh.* You've never called this time of day before."

Margo's basement *"ooooh"* had its usual affect: I was instantly wet, my insides quivering, taking my breath away. I leaned against the lamppost.

"Not now, Margo," I gasped. "This is serious."

"You can talk?"

"Yes, I can talk. The security cameras outside the Kathouse, are they on all of the time?"

"Security cameras? Yes. Why?"

"How often do you change the tapes? Do you save them?"

"Let me think. George handles the security system. I imagine they're changed daily, but don't quote me. Not sure how long we save them. A month, maybe? Why?"

"A case I'm working. I need to see if your cameras caught someone last week that I'm looking for. Can you come down here right away and let me see the tapes? It's really important."

"Okay. I'll call George and have him meet us. Say about an hour."

There were four cameras: two on the front of the building covering the sidewalk and entrance, and two on the side covering the parking lot. They had been installed back in May after the attacks. If I was really lucky, one of them may have recorded the woman I wanted to find.

As I waited for Margo and George to arrive, I walked back to get my car and tried the Loseys one more time. Still no answer. I checked my notebook and called Dr. Dorian's office number.

A woman answered. "This is Dr. Losey's service. The office is closed for the Labor Day weekend and will reopen Tuesday. How may I help you?"

"I'm trying to reach Dr. Losey."

"Is this a medical emergency?"

"No, but I need to talk with him."

"Dr. Losey is unavailable. Dr. Turner is handling his patients this week."

"I'm not a current patient, but I want to see Dr. Losey personally. How can I reach him?"

"You can't. Dr. Losey is on vacation."

"When did he leave? When will he be back?"

"He left last week and won't return until the thirteenth. However, he has no openings for new patients until mid-October. Perhaps Dr. Turner can fit you in. He has an opening Wednesday morning."

"Do you know where Dr. Losey went on vacation?"

"That information is not available. Would you like to see Dr. Turner? What is the nature of your problem?"

"Never mind."

How convenient. Stanley disappears, and Doctors Dorian and Jackie leave town. Was there a connection?

George Dunn and Margo Lane pulled into the parking lot right behind the other. Margo had been the first attack victim back in March, right here in the parking lot; George was attacked next across the road where he usually parked his car in Riverside Park. Both attacks had been late at night in ill-lit areas. When I was hired to investigate, I recommended more lighting and the cameras. Now my suggestion might pay off.

George opened up and led us back to the office.

"Margo told me what you wanted, but we don't use tapes. Everything's on computer. We have files of every moment since the system was installed. When are you looking for?"

"Last Saturday morning between 8:45 and, let's say, ten o'clock."

George pulled the dust cover off of the computer in the corner with a large flat screen monitor. He tapped the keyboard and the screen came alive. He entered a password and the screen divided into four windows showing views outside. In one window I saw our three cars in the parking lot; in another I saw the back end of my car and the rest of the empty lot. The two other windows showed the front entrance from different directions, empty sidewalk and part of the street. In the corner of each window was the current date and time.

George clicked on "Archive" at the top of the screen and entered a date in the small window that appeared. The four windows seemed to go dark; then it was night and the parking lot was full with a few people entering and leaving the front. George tapped a few more keys and sunny morning appeared: the parking lot and sidewalk were empty. The time/date in the window corners read 0845-08/28.

"Okay," George said, "who are we looking for?"

"A Japanese-American woman with long black hair wearing a grey sweatshirt, dark jeans and a Cardinals baseball cap. She was last seen about 8:50 two blocks north. I'm hoping she came this way and that your cameras caught her. She looks a lot like these photos."

"I saw those in the paper this morning. Isn't one of them wanted for murdering the other?"

"Wanted as 'a person of interest.' The murderer could be someone else with similar features. That's what I'm hoping your files will show me."

"Okay. Pull up a chair, and we'll get started. You want it real time or fast forward?"

"Fast forward, but real time whenever someone enters the picture."

I sat while Margo went and made coffee, then the three of us spent the next hour-and-a-half fruitlessly watching for my disappearing woman. The closest hit we had was the bottom half of a person in dark jeans crossing from the street onto the sidewalk at 0917. Moments later, the parking lot camera showed a man from the back with a buzz haircut wearing a tight white T-shirt as he cut across the lot. Only the one camera caught him, and we couldn't see his face. He had a rolled up bundle under his arm. We replayed the scene several times and came to the consensus that it had to be a man and not a woman with a Sinead O'Connor 'do. A homeless guy taking bottles and cans from the Kathouse's recycling bin hadn't given him a second look. We didn't think that would be the case if it had been a woman in that tight T. Wherever my woman went, she didn't come past here.

I thanked Margo and George for their time and efforts and offered to pay them; they said they owed me and asked me to stick around and have a few beers and some lunch. I was too frustrated and declined. I had to be out doing something.

Outside, I looked up and down River Drive. The woman that Jensen had seen could be anywhere. Maybe there were other security cameras in the area. Did the police know where the woman got off the bus? Had they checked for tapes? Neither Margo nor George had said anything about showing the camera files to anyone else. Should I call Frank or Montero about it? Let them know? They were pissed and anxious about finding this killer. Maybe I could get back on their good side by being a team player.

"Thanks for calling, Rachel. We already knew the woman got off at Riverside Park, but I'll pass this on to Ed. I'm pretty sure he checked for cameras in the area and came up empty on sightings, but I'll ask. We can always check again. I know this is hard on you; I know you don't want it to be Karen, but that's how it looks right now."

"Yeah, Frank, I know. But it's not her." It's not.

"Let's hope you're right. Look, you take care of yourself, and be careful about nosing around in our business. There're still thoughts out there that you're somehow involved."

"Okay, Frank. I'll be good."

There was nothing more I could do at the moment about finding Karen. I called Carter and then Danny to see if they'd heard anything from Stanley. Nothing, and I had no news for them. There was still the open question of the Doctors Losey. Maybe I could run out there and look around.

As I was being a good little team player, I called Rod's office hoping either he or Mike Carson were in, hoping they had something to tell me, and wanting to pass on the names of the Doctors Losey. It didn't matter who found Stanley, only that he be found. Of course, I got Jabba.

"What do you want?"

"Just checking in. Anything new on Stanley?"

"When there is, we'll notify the sister who filed the missing report, not you. So unless you've got something new for us—"

"No, nothing."

Fuck him, if he thought I was going to give him anything now.

I felt I was taking two steps backwards for every one forward. Every turn was either blockaded or led to a dead end. The only bright note in my day was Wendy's call. It wasn't much, but at least she agreed to see me.

My future—our future—rested on whatever happened tomorrow. What was I going to say—what could I say—to convince Wendy to give us another chance? I really needed to clear my head, make a game plan. I needed to talk to someone. But who?

I CLIMBED THE STEPS to PJs' house in Lincoln Heights. The screen was unlatched and, as usual, the front door was wide open. I heard a radio playing in the living room where four teens, one girl and three boys, were at a card table playing some kind of game with miniature figures of warriors, wizards and monsters. The girl rolled some weirdly shaped dice.

"Through the doorway the mage blasted open, you see a long, dimly lit hallway. On the floor in front of you . . ."

Across the entryway, six more teens sat around the dining table with laptop computers. Rasheena and Shoshana, PJs granddaughters who had stayed with me for several weeks following my rape, were helping them with some online project. Rasheena waved. Shoshana saw me and came over.

"Hi, Rachel. How you doing?"

We hugged. "Pretty well, I think. How about you?"

"Can't wait for classes to start."

"Is PJs here?"

"I think Grandma's out in the garden. Want me to get her?"

"I'll just go out there. Thanks. It's good to see you. Sorry I haven't been around much. I really appreciated everything you and Rasheena did for me."

"Well, don't be such a stranger. We were glad to help. Seeya."

PJs and two boys were picking tomatoes from a vegetable garden at the back of the property. PJs waved as she saw me.

"Rachel, dear, how nice of you to visit."

"Hi. I was wondering if you had a free moment to talk?"

"Certainly. Just a moment. Jason, would you take this basket in, please, and bring Rachel and me a pitcher of tea over by the table? Thank you. Brad, could you pick about two dozen or so nice green tomatoes? We can fry them later for supper. Thank you."

PJs and I went over to a set of table and chairs in the shade of an apple tree.

"We haven't seen you in nearly two months, Rachel. How are you doing?"

What to say? How much to tell her?

"My recovery's slower than expected. And I've met someone. Someone special."

Once I started, the words poured out of me. I only paused when Jason brought the tea and waited for him to go help Brad. Without graphic detail, I told PJs about Wendy and I becoming budding lovers and how I had hurt her; about finding Carter and the flashbacks of my rape; about searching for Stanley and my ill-timed affair with Danny; about Karen being back and accused of terrible crimes, but not being able to find her; about Wendy wanting to see me, but being afraid of how I might win or lose her.

"What am I going to do?"

PJs shook her head slowly. "You don't do things by halves, do you? Tell me, this: do you still love Karen?

"Yes, but I don't know if she still loves me or where she's at or why she returned."

"Do you love Wendy?"

"Yes, but I don't know if she'll forgive me."

"Do you love Danny?"

"No. I like her. I want to help her find her brother, but I don't love her. I don't want to sleep with, or use her, again."

"Rachel, I'm not sure how to advise you. Karen and Wendy don't seem to be women who would want to share affections. You say Karen can't be the murderer everyone is looking for, but what if she is? Will you stand by her? Take the chance of losing Wendy?"

"I'm not sure."

"It sounds to me like Wendy wants you despite how you've hurt her. You need to make a choice, and I can't make it for you."

I nodded. "I know. Thanks for listening. I'm not sure

what I'm going to do, but talking to you has helped."

Twenty

As I LEFT THE HOUSE, Jennifer, one of the young teens staying there and who helped me find Linda Miller back in May, came storming angrily down the sidewalk. She climbed the porch steps without noticing me. Her eyes were puffy from crying, and she was muttering, "Stupid! Stupid! Stupid!"

"Hi, Jen. What's wrong?"

"Oh, hi, Miss Cord. I didn't see you. I need to see PJs right away."

"Can I help?"

"I don't know? I don't know what to do."

"Tell me about it, and maybe we can figure something out."

Jennifer looked down at her feet, thinking; then looked at me.

"It's Barbara. She's being stupid. Stupid! Stupid! Stupid!"

Barbara was Jen's older friend who had also helped find Linda.

"What's she done that's so stupid?"

"She's gonna get in trouble. That's what."

"How?"

"She went with a man! She knows better. I told her not to. She'll get hurt." Jennifer started crying again. "I know she will."

"What man? Where? When? Jen, answer me."

"She made me promise not to tell."

"As you said, she's in trouble. Who is he?"

"Some guy we met. Derek something. She went to his motel room. Half an hour ago, I think. What time is it?"

"It's 2:50."

"Half an hour, then."

"Do you know what motel?"

"The Sunrise Motel on Cutter. He took her to room 262. It's in the back. I saw it."

"Let's go!"

"Where?"

"To get her back."

I turned my car around and headed for Cutter Avenue as fast as I could.

"Where'd you meet this guy? How old is he?"

"At the food court at the mall. He must be forty, at least."

"How did you and Barbara connect with him?"

"I'm not sure. When we got to the mall, it was as if Barb was looking for someone."

"Did he approach you guys?"

"No. We circled the food court a couple of times and then Barb said, 'over there.'"

"Then what happened?"

"They talked. He bought us sodas and burgers. Then he drove us to the motel. That's when Barb made me promise, and they went upstairs."

"What kind of car was it?"

"Dark green, four doors, pretty new."

"Okay, hold on while I make a call."

I scrolled though the numbers on my cell phone as I made the turn on to Cutter.

"Sgt. Trujillo, how may I help you?"

"Kerri, it's Rachel Cord. How fast can you get to the Sunrise Motel on Cutter Avenue?"

"Why?"

"There's a pedophile there right now with a fifteen-year-old girl, and—"

"Barb's fourteen," Jennifer said.

"Make that fourteen. And I don't think they're having a tea party. I'm headed there to intervene and having you there would sure help."

"It may take me twenty minutes, but I can have a unit there in five. Do you know the room number?"

"Two sixty-two. It's around the back. The man's name is Derek, no last name, about forty. The guy drives a late-model, dark green sedan. Don't have the make or plate yet. I'm nearly there now."

"I'm on my way. Don't do anything foolish. Wait for the unit to arrive."

A minute later I pulled into the Sunrise Motel and drove around back. Jennifer pointed out the car. I parked blocking it.

"Stay in the car. When the police arrive, send them up."

"What are you going to do?"

"Stop whatever's happening in that room."

I ran up the stairs. The curtains to room 262 were closed and a "Do Not Disturb" sign hung on the doorknob. I looked out over the rail, but didn't see any police yet. I leaned against the door and could faintly hear voices, but not what was being said. Several doors down, a housekeeping cart sat in front of an open room. I glanced in that room and heard the housekeeper cleaning the bathroom. On top of the cart's trash basket was a copy of today's *Daily Record*. I grabbed the paper as I pushed the cart down to 262 so that it could be seen from the windows.

I rolled the first section of the newspaper into a tight cylinder. It wouldn't be as effective as a rolled up magazine but was better than nothing. I knocked on the door.

"Housekeeping." I waited a moment and knocked again. "Housekeeping. We need to get in, please."

"Go away," a man said. "Can't you see the sign?"

"Yes, sir. I saw the sign. I'm sorry, sir, for the inconvenience, but we do need to get in."

I was making it up as I went along. I had no idea if this room had been done earlier, or what the policy was.

"This is the Housekeeping supervisor. Local ordinances require us to physically check all rooms daily."

"Can't you come back later?"

"Sorry, sir, but the staff is due to leave shortly. This will just take a moment."

"Just a minute."

I looked quickly over the rail. Still no police. As I turned back, I saw the curtain move slightly. The door lock clicked and the door opened part way.

As Jennifer had said, the man, Derek Something, was about 40 and a couple of inches taller than me. He had dark hair and rugged features in a "Marlboro Man" kind of way.

"I still don't see why you couldn't do this—"

"I understand, sir. I'm truly sorry. We'll be as quick as possible."

I pushed the door fully open and jammed the rolled up newspaper into Derek's gut as hard as I could, pushing him back into the room.

"Hey! That hurts."

"Not as much as it's going too. Where's my daughter!" I screamed as loud as I could.

"Dau . . . daughter? What daughter? There's no one here."

"Don't tell me she's not here, you pervert! Barbara! Barbara!"

"Quiet down, for christsakes, you bitch. There's no one here, I tell you."

"Like hell there isn't!" I banged on the bathroom door. "Barbara! I know you're in there. You come out right this instant."

"There's no one here. Will you get out of—"

I pointed the paper at him. "You stay back." I banged the

bathroom door again. "Barbara, darling. It's okay. You can come home. I kicked Stanley out. Come home to momma, baby."

"You're not my mother! Go away!"

I turned on Derek. "What did you do to her that she disclaims her *own* mother? How dare you! Beast!"

"Look, lady. Get out of here before I call the cops."

"Yes! Call the cops! I want the cops. Pervert! Pervert!"

"What's going on here?"

Two uniformed police officers stood at the door.

The man turned pale, but pointed at me. "This crazy woman broke into my room."

I threatened him again with the paper. "This pedophile has a fourteen-year-old he picked up at the mall in his bathroom." I knocked on the bathroom door. "Barbara, it's okay, now. The police are here. You can come out."

The officers came into the room.

Derek backed away. "This woman's crazy. My daughter and I are here on vacation. This woman broke in and threatened us. My daughter ran into the bathroom to get away from her."

"That's not true."

"Ma'am," the first officer held out his hand. "Put the stick down and step away from the bathroom."

"It's only a newspaper." I let it unroll, dropped it and stepped back. "I'm Rachel Cord, a private detective. Detective Trujillo from Sex Crimes is on her way here now. She called you guys."

Derek edged toward the door. The other officer standing there held up his hand. "Sir, why don't you go sit over there."

"The woman's crazy, I tell you. She came in screaming that my daughter was hers. Threatened both of us. She jabbed me—"

"Sir. Sit down and be quiet."

Derek sat in a chair in the corner by the window. I moved carefully over to the dresser and sat on it next to the TV. I kept my hands in plain sight. The two officers didn't know the situation, and I didn't want them overreacting to anything. The first officer knocked on the bathroom door.

"This is Officer Palumbo, city police. Open the door, please."

"No."

"Are you all right? Are you injured?"

"I'm fine. Make that woman go away. She's not my mother."

Officer Palumbo looked at me.

"It's true. She's not my daughter. She's not his either. Barbara stays at PJs Johnson's home in Lincoln Heights. I think she met this creep on the Internet and hooked up at the mall."

Officer Palumbo turned back to the door. "Barbara? Is that your name? I need you to open the door. I need to know that you're all right."

"Make her go away. Leave us alone. Derek hasn't done anything."

"Babs!" Derek yelled. "You can come out. Daddy's okay."

"Sir," the officer at the door said. "I asked you to be quiet."

The two officers looked at each other and shook their heads. Officer Palumbo looked at me, again. I shrugged.

"I'm just waiting for Detective Trujillo."

"Someone using my name in vain?"

Detective Sergeant Kerri Trujillo appeared at the door. Another uniformed officer towered behind her. Today, she wore a tailored pastel pantsuit that set off her dark hair and eyes and brown skin. Her shield and ID hung from a cord about her neck. Since meeting and working with her months back, I always thought it a shame that she was married and not bent the right way. Kerri is only five-three but there's never a doubt when she's in charge.

"Okay. What's happening here?"

"This woman—" Derek closed his mouth and sat back

down when the officer beside him held up his hand.

Officer Palumbo stepped forward. "I'm Officer Palumbo and my partner is Officer Drury. We got a report of a suspected pedophile at this location with an under-aged girl. When we arrived, we heard loud voices, the door was open, and this man and woman were arguing. The woman was trying to get the girl locked in the bathroom to come out. The girl says she's all right and that nothing has happened, but I haven't been able to get her to open the door. The man claims to be her father, but the girl called him by his first name. The woman says the man and girl hooked up at the mall and came here. She also says that she's a private dick and that she called you. That's about it, so far."

Kerri nodded. "She is and she did." She turned toward Derek. "You don't have to say anything, sir, if you don't want to, but it might expedite things if you do. What's your story?"

"My daughter and I are here on vacation before school starts. Yes, we were at the mall before coming back here. We were talking about going out to dinner when this woman claiming to be 'housekeeping' knocked on the door. When I opened it, she pushed her way in and attacked me. Then she started screaming that Babs was her daughter and calling me a pervert. I've never seen the woman before in my life. Babs locked herself in the bathroom for safety. You should arrest that woman. She's crazy."

"You say she attacked you. Did she have a weapon?"

"Some kind of club, I think."

Kerri looked at me. I pointed to the unrolled newspaper lying on the floor. Officer Palumbo picked it up and handed it to Kerri.

"She hit you with a newspaper?"

"It didn't feel like a newspaper."

"Right. May I see some identification, please?"

"Ah . . . sure." Derek stood, took out his wallet. He gave Kerri his driver's license.

"Victor H. Lamb, Oklahoma City, Oklahoma. Is this your

correct name and current address?"

"Yes."

"The girl called him Derek," Officer Palumbo said.

"Is that right? Why is that, Mr. Lamb?"

"Ah . . . It's a pet name. I work on oilrigs. Derricks."

"Uh-huh. Thank you. Please sit, and remain quiet. Rachel, what do you say?"

"Pretty much what I told you on the phone. This guy calling himself Derek picked Barbara up at the mall and brought her here. Barbara stays with PJs over in Lincoln Heights. I was there when Barbara's friend Jennifer showed up crying. She told me what happened and we drove here as I called you. When we got here, the police hadn't arrived. Afraid of what might be happening in this room, I used a ruse to gain entry to stall for time and keep any harm from occurring to Barbara. When I came in, Barbara was already locked in the bathroom. Shortly thereafter, officers Palumbo and Drury arrived."

"Is Jennifer the girl downstairs?"

"Yes. I told her to wait in the car and tell the police which room to come to."

Kerri turned to the officer who arrived with her. "Matt, go downstairs and talk with Jennifer. Get her story. Tell her that her friend's okay. Mr. Lamb, do you have anything you want to add at this time?"

"Ah, just that this is all a big misunderstanding. Ah . . ."

"I think I understand. Thank you. Officer Drury would you take Mr. Lamb outside, please. Go down the landing a few doors. I'll call when I want him back. Mr. Lamb, please go with the officer. I'll try to speak with Barbara and see if we can get this all sorted out."

Drury and Lamb left the room and Kerri knocked on the bathroom door.

"Barbara, this is Detective Kerri Trujillo, city police. Are you all right? Barbara?"

"I'm fine."

"Would you open the door, please, so that we can talk?"

"What have you done to Derek? Is he all right?"

"He's fine. He's outside with one of my officers. Nothing's happened to him. Would you please come out?"

"Is Rachel still there?"

"Yes."

"Make her leave, too."

"Officer Palumbo, please escort Ms. Cord outside and stay with her."

As the door closed behind us, I heard Kerri say, "Okay, Barbara, it's just you and me now. You can—"

I saw Derek, George Lamb, that is, several doors down with Officer Drury leaning against the rail. I looked down at the parking lot where Jennifer sat on the hood of my car. I didn't see the officer who went down to speak with her. Jennifer waved and I waved back. A few minutes passed and that officer came along the landing and stood with Palumbo and me. His nametag said Bates. Some time later, the door opened and Kerri stepped out. Bates motioned to her and they went farther down the landing and spoke. When they came back, Kerri motioned to Drury and Lamb.

"Mr. Lamb. I've spoken with Barbara and Officer Bates has spoken with the girl downstairs and the motel management. Management says that you checked in alone. Do you still claim that Barbara is your daughter?"

"Ah . . ."

"Are you willing to provide a DNA sample to prove that?"

"Ah . . . This is really a misunderstanding. Can't we just—"

"Mr. Lamb, will you give us permission to search your room and car?"

"Ah . . . Maybe I should talk to a lawyer?"

"Maybe you should. Mr. Lamb, please place your hands behind you. Officer Palumbo, please handcuff him. George Lamb, we are arresting you for child endangerment. Please know that other charges may be made pending our investigation. Officers, please complete the arrest, advise Mr. Lamb of his rights and take him downtown."

"You gonna arrest her too? She attacked me, you know."

"With a newspaper, I remember. I'll handle it, thank you."

Palumbo, Drury and Lamb left.

"You hit him with a newspaper?"

"Poked him, actually, to get him to back away from the door."

"Save it for your statement. Matt, secure the room and wait until we get a warrant out here for a search of the room and car. I particularly want to find his laptop. I'll also contact Oklahoma for a search there." Kerri opened the motel room door. "Barbara, it's time to go."

Barbara came out of the room. She wouldn't look at or speak to me. Bates locked the room as Barbara, Kerri and I headed for the stairs. Kerri took Barbara with her, and Jennifer and I followed them to the police station. After we gave and signed statements, Kerri warned me that Lamb might pursue an assault charge but didn't think much would come of it.

"He's got enough problems of his own right now."

I took Barbara and Jennifer to PJs. Jennifer ran up the stairs and into the house. Barbara stopped on the bottom step and turned.

"I'm sorry, Miss Cord. I was stupid."

"I'm just glad that you're okay."

Twenty-One

AFTER LEAVING BARBARA and Jennifer, I wasted the afternoon seeking leads on either Karen or Stanley. I still felt that the Loseys could help me; that they might be the answer to locating Stanley. It seemed too much of a coincidence that they left town about the same time Stanley disappeared. I decided to drive out to their place and look around.

The Doctors Losey lived in one of the older, but desirable, neighborhoods on the north side. Mature trees lined the wide street. The house, a two-and-a-half-story brick Victorian, sat above the street on a double lot. I climbed the steps of the walkway and up onto the porch and rang the bell. There was no answer. I hadn't expected to find anyone home. The Doctors were on vacation somewhere, and no one had answered my phone calls.

It was early evening when everything is graying and it's difficult to see, but the streetlights hadn't come on yet. It's a time when families are sitting down to dinner or getting ready to go out, a time that people don't expect burglars in the neighborhood. Hanging plants, columns, and porch rails screened me in deep shadow from prying eyes. Breaking and entering is not my idea of a good time, and I had no idea if I would find anything to help me locate Stanley, but it was the only idea I had.

I put on a pair of gloves and was inserting the tip of my lockpick gun into the front door lock when an airport limousine pulled up in front of the house. The driver opened the back door and a woman and man got out. They were casually dressed, and each carried a soft leather duffel bag. I recognized Dr. Jackie from the videotape. The driver began unloading luggage from the trunk. I put the lockpick gun and gloves back in my bag and stepped to the front of the porch.

"Hello," the woman said. "Are you waiting for us?"

"Yes, I am, if you're Doctors Losey."

"Well, aren't you lucky? We hadn't planned to be home for another week. That's a long wait. What can we do for you?"

"I'm Rachel Cord. I'm a private investigator. I'm looking for information on a friend of yours."

"We're not tattletales. Who might that be?"

"Kenneth Stanley."

"I don't believe we know a Kenneth Stanley. Do we, dear?"

She was very smooth. He wasn't quite so convincing.

"No. No, I don't believe we do. Sorry."

"I have a videotape with me that indicates otherwise."

His eyes widened, but she gave me an amused closed-mouth smile. I could almost see the feathers peeking out from the corner of her mouth.

"I see. Perhaps you should come in. You won't mind waiting until we dispose of the driver, will you?"

The front room was quite nice. Hardwood floors with oriental rugs, lace curtains at the windows, high ceiling with fan, comfortable nineteenth-century sofas and winged-back chairs, oiled landscapes on the pale-green walls.

The Doctors looked athletically trim and younger than their ages, although his hairline was retreating rapidly; her hair was long and dark without a hint of gray. Did she color it?

"I'm Jackie. This is Dorian. May we call you 'Rachel'?"

"That's fine."

"Please, Rachel, make yourself comfortable. Would you like some sherry, or wine? Or something else?" She opened a cabinet exposing a complete bar. Bottles of Glenfiddich, Lagavulin and Laphroaig tempted from one of the shelves, Grey Goose from another.

"Nothing, thank you."

She filled two tumblers with sherry and ice and joined her husband on a sofa. They seemed completely at ease.

"You said you have a videotape. I hope this isn't an attempt at blackmail."

"It isn't blackmail. I'm looking for information. You don't seem surprised about the videotape."

"Not at all. Stan is always making videos. Impossible not to notice, unless one is too high or too drunk or," she paused slightly and smiled, "too involved. Stan makes them for his personal pleasure. I think they're fun. How did you get one of them?"

"Stanley is missing. I've been hired to find him. I found his tape collection at his house. You've been out of town since he disappeared. Was he with you?"

"No. We haven't seen Stan in weeks. What happened to him?"

"No one knows. He ate breakfast last Saturday near work, but never made it across the parking lot to his job. The police are now looking for him. Would you have any idea where he might be?"

"None at all. We flew to Miami on the twenty-sixth for some fun and a cruise, but cut short our trip because of the hurricane. It was a madhouse trying to find a flight back. We finally opted to rent a car and drive to Atlanta and fly from there. The traffic was awful, but we beat the weather. I'm exhausted. I hope Stan is all right. He's fun. How did you find us from the tapes?"

"Gordon gave me your names and address."

"Ah, Gordon; a very pleasing young man. Dorian's quite fond of him; almost as much as Stan is, aren't you dear?" She placed her hand on his crotch. "Tell me, Rachel, did you find the tapes interesting? Shall we watch this one?"

"I'm more the private, one-woman-at-a-time, type. Do you know any of the other participants?"

"Not really. We only go there a few times a year. Most use phony names or nicknames which is silly and hypocritical, but that's the way life is, isn't it? Stan liked variety. So do we. That's part of the fun. There were hardly any regulars except for Gordon."

"What about Scotty?" Dorian asked.

"Who's Scotty?"

"Another favorite of Dorian's," Jackie smiled as she ran her hand over his thigh. "And Stan's. I'm sure that's not his real name."

"Why do you think that?"

"I'm not sure. Maybe it's the way Stan always used it when the two of them were going to have sex. He'd say, 'Beam me up, Scotty,' very lecherously. It always produced a laugh for the rest of us. It's as if it were Stan's pet name for him."

"I think he's of Scottish descent," said Dorian, "but I never heard his real name either."

"And he was a regular?"

Jackie sipped her sherry. "Quite often when we were there. I couldn't speak of the times we weren't."

"Has he ever been here?"

"No, unfortunately. Although we have invited him."

"When did you last see him?"

"Last week in July, I think. Isn't that right, dear?"

"Yes. That's the last time we were at Stan's."

"Do you know what he does for a living?"

"I'm afraid not. That's a subject that doesn't come up in these gatherings."

"What does he look like?"

"Young, blond with Paul Newman blue eyes." Jackie smiled her bird-eating smile. "And as well endowed below the waist as you are above."

I felt a blush coming. "Would he be on the tapes?"

"I shouldn't be surprised. Shall we see?"

I gave her the tape. She was itching to see it. She opened a cabinet containing a TV, DVD player and VCR. We played the tape. They seemed to like it, but it was no help to me.

Jackie paused the tape the second time through. "That may be him, but I can't be certain."

There was a blurred image of the back of a head between her legs. The hair may have been blond, but it could have been the lighting. I had cut the scene right at that point.

"Pity you can't see more. You missed a lot of fun action. You should have copied the whole thing instead of bits and snips of us. Have the police seen the originals?"

"I presume so. I told them about them, and they've searched the house."

No point in saying that the tapes were missing. Damn it. Why didn't I take them?

"They've also interviewed Gordon."

"Then I imagine they'll be contacting us also. Perhaps we should call them first. What do you think?"

"That would be a good idea."

I wrote the number on the back of my card and gave it to her.

"Ask for either detective Carson or Jablowski. One more thing: do you know Karen Tanaka?"

Dorian shook his head "no." Jackie gave it more thought.

"Associate professor in the Art Department. We met occasionally but she left Cramer last year about this time, I think. Why? Is she another of Stan's friends?"

"Not that I know of. When did you last see her?"

"God, it's been a while. Let me think. It was last year some time. It must have been mid or late August, before the start of the fall semester. She arranged a display of paintings and sculpture for our department. Several were hers, I believe. The display is still there. I haven't seen her since."

Jackie returned the tape and walked me to the door.

"Sorry, we couldn't be of more help. I really do hope Stan is all right."

"So do I, but it's been a week since anyone's heard from him. That's not a good sign. Tell me, Dorian's middle initial is W; is his name Wayne?"

"No, it's William. Why?"

"Just a curiosity. Stan's middle name is Wayne, and I've come across several others recently."

"How odd. My maiden name is Wayne, and I often use it as a middle name."

She smiled and lightly caressed my arm. Goosebumps made me shiver.

"Perhaps we should get together and discuss it. Just the two of us, of course."

Twenty-Two

MY DAY WAS A BUST, and I spent the rest of the night fretting about what to say to Wendy, what she might decide, and what I should wear to please her. I was so frazzled that at 3:00 AM — still undecided and amazingly hadn't hit the bottle of Glenfiddich — I forgot about Margo and our usual late night *Voice* ecstasy.

At five minutes to 11:00 the next morning, I nervously stood on the dock in front of the South Ferry Transportation Company, an upscale restaurant and area icon on a restored ferry moored at the end of Cutter Avenue and the river. The original South Ferry Company dates back to when ferries were the only way to cross the river. It started as little more than a large raft on a towline dragged across the river by mule. Railroad and, later, highway bridges made ferries obsolete, but South Ferry somehow stayed in business until the 1950s. The ferry gave the community its name, and even when the city enveloped it nearly a century ago, the name stuck for the district.

The last ferry, a grand three-decker with the bottom deck for vehicles, an enclosed second deck for passengers and the third an open deck and bridge, sat sunk in the mud for decades until investors raised it in '84 and created a marvelous restaurant. Now, once a month, throughout the summer, the fully restored ferry is taken out on the river for special — although pricey — events. Karen and I went once; we had a great time and a wonderful memory. Today's brunch would be the last trip of the season. What memories would it bring?

A horn split the air announcing pending departure. Dozens of people continued to pass me and go up the entryway. I'd been there 10 or 15 minutes twisting one way and another deciding what to do. I felt foolish. At least I had finally settled on something to wear: a yellow and white summer frock, full-skirted, short sleeved, modest yoke neckline, a broad-brimmed white summer straw hat, bag to match, shawl for cool breezes, white shoes and gloves (badly twisted from nervous wringing) and a single strand of pearls. Very unlike me who prefers trousers and altered men's jackets, but I was trying for June Alyson or Donna Reed instead of Hepburn or Dietrich as Marlowe. I was scared of failure, of being rejected, of losing something precious. I nearly turned and walked away — better to run now than be rejected later — when I saw Wendy at the rail of the upper deck watching me.

How long she stood there watching, I had no idea. Her long hair blew freely in the breeze. It reminded me of my picture of Karen standing at that same railing, but this wasn't the time to think of Karen.

Wendy wore a two-piece cream-colored suit and a lighter scoop-necked blouse; a glimmer of gold around her neck was some kind of jewelry but I couldn't tell what from that distance. She didn't smile or wave but turned her head as if nodding toward the gangway. I took a deep breath, shyly waved and went on board.

We met at the restaurant entrance on the second deck as the final whistle blew and the ferry moved out onto the river. I nervously smoothed the wrinkles of my gloves. I felt a lump in my throat as I saw that the jewelry Wendy wore on a gold chain was a cameo. Did she remember the cameos worn at Phil's? Was she trying to tell me that she was available? That we had a chance? Her cool green eyes offered no clue. She hadn't spoken, and I wasn't sure where to start.

I could have started with a simple "thank you for inviting me." When I came aboard, the ticket taker checked off my name and refused my credit card saying it was taken care of already. So a "thank you" would have been an appropriate icebreaker, but even that wouldn't squeak out.

The maitre d' showed us to a window table for two and removed the "Reserved" sign. A waiter offered us various juices or mimosas—champagne and orange juice with a touch of grenadine—as he placed a bowl of strawberries and sliced kiwi sprinkled with blueberries and a basket of mini scones on the table. We chose the mimosas.

If this were a celebration date, we could toast each other, but that was yet to be determined. Wendy stared out the window at the passing scenery. I glanced about the room. We weren't ready to speak. Many people still wandered in and were being seated. Dress was highly varied: from casual shorts and shirts to high couture. Only a few women wore gloves; mostly regulars that I recognized from Phil's.

Large trolleys began circling the room carrying an abundant array of food. One of the many unique things about South Ferry's brunch buffets was that you didn't have to stand in line at tables to make your choices; the buffet came to you.

There were trolleys loaded with mincemeat sticky buns, coffeecakes, biscuits, muffins, scones, Danish, cornbread, and apple, blueberry, strawberry and peach turnovers. Several trolleys made waffles and pancakes fresh at your table, or omelets made to order. Others were loaded with various sausages, bacons, carved-to-order ham and prime rib, or smoked salmon, haddock and herring. Still others carried savory quiches, some made with tofu instead of egg, and stratas and frittatas. This was dieter's hell.

I removed my gloves and turned back just as Wendy did.

Impulsively I held up my mimosa as if making a toast.

"I just want to say two things. First, I made mistakes. I can't undo them, or pretend they didn't happen. I regret them, and . . . I'm sorry I hurt you. I never wanted to hurt you. Second, I . . . I . . ." I love you. I want you in my life, my messy life. I want to hold you, love you, be yours forever. "Second, I, no matter what, I want to be your friend."

Wendy's lips curled slightly into a dubious smile.

"I still don't want you as a friend. But I've made mistakes too. I presumed too much, too soon. I'm a banker. I should know better. I study assets, liabilities. Credits, debits. Accounts payable, accounts receivable. Everything in order, everything weighed. Bottom line: in the black? Or in the red? And yet, I jumped into this like a naïve investor not knowing anything. It was unfair. I'm sorry too."

Wendy looked at the glass that I had forgotten I was still holding up.

"Are you making a proposal?"

The double meaning made me blush.

"Yes. That is . . . I don't expect a do-over, but, I mean . . . Friends!"

I held my glass out.

Wendy pursed her lips, shook her head and then clinked her glass to mine.

"More."

My heart skipped and the lump in my throat made it hard to swallow.

"More."

The mood lightened, and we indulged in the banquet. Wendy had Eggs Diablo, *Huevos escalfado Diablo*, South Ferry's signature version of Eggs Benedict: two eggs perfectly poached in Tabasco laid on a circle of grilled polenta and crumbled chorizo covered in a tomatillo/cilantro sauce. *¡Muy caliente!* I chose a less fiery Egg Benedict salad: poached egg on a salad of frisée, shelled edamame, sliced radish, sliced red onion, crumbled crisp prosciutto and crumbled Gorgonzola drizzled with Hollandaise.

Over a shared waffle covered with fresh strawberries and whipped cream, we talked more about each other's past, about where we were in our lives. Then we went topside to enjoy the view and escape the food temptations. We had another mimosa and continued talking. Later we went back and shared a Vietnamese-style barbequed five-spice chicken sandwich with marinated daikon and a citrus salad of oranges and grapefruit with star anise syrup; then topside again with more mimosas.

As the ferry returned to the dock, I looked at Wendy and did the Groucho thing with my eyebrows.

"Want to see my Munch again?"

Wendy laughed. "Dibs for on top. That linoleum's cold."

Twenty-Three

LABOR DAY MORNING started bright and clear. A good day for picnics, barbeques and other fun activities. Wendy was wrapped in my terry robe, and I wore a light peignoir as we had coffee on the balcony. She reached out and took my hand.

"Rachel, this is crazy."

"What is?"

"My being here with you. You're so much younger."

"Age doesn't mean anything."

"Yes, it does. And it scares me. It's part of why I was so hurt. Karen's your age, and Sarah was what? Early twenties? And Danny? How can I compete with that?"

"Nine years. It's nothing. There are lots of successful relationships like that. My parents, for instance. Just give us a chance."

Wendy shook her head, then leaned over and kissed me.

"Okay. It scares me, but okay. And you need to understand something else. I've always been monogamous. I want to be with you, I really do, but I don't want to be a sometime thing or part of a threesome or a foursome or whatever. It may be selfish, but I prefer to be an only. Can you understand that?"

"Yes. I—"

The doorbell rang.

"Who's that?

"I've no idea."

The bell rang again as I went to the door. I saw Frank Taylor through the peephole.

"Frank, what are you doing here?"

"Let me in, Rachel. We need to speak."

"Just a moment, I'm not dressed."

I went back to Wendy. "It's Frank. Something's up."

We went to the bedroom and I pulled on a pair of sweats and went to open the door.

"Frank, I don't know where Karen is. She's not here."

"I know that. Rachel—"

"Frank, really, I don't—"

"Rachel, dear? Please let us in. Detective Taylor has something important to say."

"PJs? Shoshana?" I hadn't seen them standing behind Frank. "What are you doing here?"

"Let's go sit inside, Rachel."

I moved backward as Frank, PJs and Shoshana entered. I followed them to the dining table.

"What's going on?"

PJs pulled out a chair. "Rachel, you better sit down."

"Why? What's happened? Did you catch Karen? Is she all right?"

"Please, Rachel," PJs said. "Please sit down."

I could see tears welling in Shoshana's eyes. I sat. Frank took a plastic evidence bag from his pocket.

"Do you recognize this?"

I held the bag. Inside was a gold ankle chain with two interlaced open hearts. One heart was engraved with the initial K, the other with R. I had given it to Karen on our first anniversary. I began to shake.

"Where, where did you get this?"

"Another woman's body was found buried yesterday."

"No." I shook my head vigorously. "This was by the body?"

"It was on her left ankle."

"No. No."

"The body's been there about a year."

"No."

My head moved back and forth. I was cold. Someone hugged me. I felt hot tears on my neck.

"I'm sorry, Rachel. We're awaiting dental records for positive identification, but blood types match. It appears Karen was also a victim; not the woman we're looking for, after all."

I stopped listening, closed my eyes. I knew Frank was talking, but I didn't hear anything else he said. I leaned into the comforting arms around me. Karen was dead. She'd been dead for a year. She hadn't run out on me. All this time I thought . . . Oh, god. I opened my eyes. Across the table PJs looked gravely concerned. Tears ran down Shoshana's cheeks. I suddenly realized it was Wendy who held me, comforted me. She must have dressed and come from the bedroom. I hugged her and turned to Frank.

"If Karen's . . . then who was that in Florida?"

"We don't know; presumably her killer posing as Karen. The same person who killed Aiko Nagasawa and the others. That's something else we discovered."

"What?"

"The killer takes over her victims' identities, moves away to some place where she or the victims aren't known, and then lives as them for a period of time. Lockhart interviewed one of the many callers we got on our alert. A woman who said she knew Evelyn Martinez. They were neighbors here for six months in '98 before she said that Martinez suddenly cut out on her lease and left a lot of bills. She even owed this woman several hundred dollars. Of course, this was after the real Martinez was dead, and everyone thought she had run away from California.

"Someone else gave us a lead on the unknown woman's body. Angela Ohara. Same story. Suddenly ups and leaves town without a word to friends or family. Cancels utilities and puts mail on hold. Nine months later over in Kansas, she completely disappears again with overdrawn bank accounts and maxed-out credit. Meanwhile, the real Ohara has been dead and buried here the whole time."

"That's what she was going to do with Nagasawa, isn't it? Take over her identity?"

"We think so. It was just chance that she was seen burying the body."

"So where is she? Who is she?"

"We don't know. From leads, we've interviewed three more women who look a lot like Karen and the others. None could possibly have done these crimes."

"But they could be potential victims, if this woman isn't caught."

"One of them at least. This woman picks on single women, without immediate families. Two of the women we've interviewed have husbands and children. The thing is, we don't know how or where she meets her targets. I don't know if we'll catch her or not. With the current publicity she may have left town already."

"Can I see her? Karen, I mean."

"She's been buried a year, Rachel. You wouldn't recognize her. You don't want to see that."

"Yes, I do. I have to." I need to apologize.

"Technically you're not next of kin. Except for this ankle bracelet, there's no way to make a visual ID. It wouldn't be authorized."

"Frank, please. I really need to see her."

"I'll see what I can do. I'll call you later."

"Thanks. Has her family been notified?"

"Not yet. We're waiting on the dental ID. Probably tomorrow."

"I'll call Tori, her sister. Give her a heads-up."

Frank left. PJs and Shoshana stayed and I introduced them to Wendy. Shoshana made fresh coffee as PJs and Wendy spoke quietly together. I went to the bookcase and got Karen's picture, her impish smile full of life. I held the picture against me and wandered into Karen's studio gallery.

Karen was still here. Every brushstroke on every painting was a bit of Karen. I remembered again posing for her, our making love. Forgive me, Karen. Please forgive me. How could I have doubted you? Distrusted you? How could I not be sure that that woman wasn't you?

Helen had said, *Frankly, I don't know what you saw in that woman. Maybe she changed. She was very cold and aloof when I saw her. Nervous, too. Made me think she was hiding something."*

Yes. She was hiding something. That she wasn't Karen. That she'd killed Karen, stolen her identity. Now she was back here and had killed again. Can the police find her? Can I?

"Rachel?"

I turned and Wendy came and hugged me.

"When I said I wanted you all to myself, this isn't what I meant. I'm sorry about Karen."

"I know." I held Wendy tightly to me. "I know."

"I'm going home to change and pack a bag. I'll be back as soon as I can. PJs and Shoshana will stay with you."

"I'll be fine."

"Shoshana's making you some breakfast. Eat something. You're sure you're okay?"

"Yes. Yes. I'm okay. Now go, but hurry back."

Twenty-Four

"ARE YOU SURE YOU don't want me to stay?" Wendy sipped her coffee and was dressed for work.

"I'll be fine. I have some calls to make. Go to work."

"Meet me for lunch?"

"Okay. Twelve-thirty at Phil's. All right?"

"That'll be good. Are you sure? I can call and say I'm not coming in. No problem."

"Go to work."

Wendy left, and I wasn't so sure. I was wracked with guilt and rage. I—

My phone rang.

"Hi, this is Mike. Detective Carson. I just got off the phone with Jackie and Dorian Losey. Thanks for having them call us."

"Were they any help?"

"Possibly. Gave me a couple of ideas. But what's this about a tape you showed them? I thought you didn't take any tapes from Stanley's house."

Oh-oh. "I made a tape of scenes that the Loseys were in from Stanley's collection. I thought it'd give me an edge in talking to them. I didn't take the originals. They should have been there when you looked. I'm sorry now I didn't take them. Then we'd have them now. The cuts I made didn't show other people well enough to ID. The tape's worthless."

"How about you bring it to us, and we decide if it's worth anything or not."

"I can do that."

"How soon?"

"Tomorrow?"

"Today. ASAP."

"Today's not good. I've gotten some bad news."

"Sorry to hear that, but we need that tape. You want this guy found or not?"

"I do. I really do. It's just that—"

"Rachel. Bring us the tape. Now."

"I'm not ready to leave just yet, and the tape's at my office. Give me a couple of hours. There may be traffic."

"Okay, I'll be expecting you. Anything else you're keeping from us?"

"No, and I've run out of ideas. What are you doing?"

"While I'm waiting for that tape from you? Not sure. Maybe I'll have another talk with MacPherson based on what the Loseys told me."

The waitress? "MacPherson? What's she got to do with it?"

"She? Don't you mean he?"

"He? Who? She's a waitress at IHOP."

"That's his wife. I'm talking about Cameron MacPherson, the guy from the shoe store."

"Cameron? The Loseys didn't mention him to me."

"They didn't give me his name exactly, but with a name like Cameron MacPherson, I'm betting that he's the one they call Scotty. Now bring us that tape."

Cameron is Scotty? Scotty is a frequent player. Cameron said he only . . . He lied to me. Cameron's a born-again with a new wife. A very religious new wife.

"*I pray for him,*" Jeannie had said. Not "I will pray." Could she and Cameron have . . .

I hurriedly dressed and went to my office. Doris reminded me that I had an appointment at 2:00 with Mavis Webb.

"Thanks. I had forgotten about it. See you later."

I got the tape, loaded my gun, took a speedloader with an extra five rounds, and headed for the river. Traffic was light, luckily, and I crossed the river in record time. But I wasn't headed to give Carson the tape right away. I was going to the MacPherson home first.

I drove past the house. The curtains were closed like the last time I was there. The black van was gone. I parked a few houses down and walked back. I walked up the drive instead of to the front door trying to look into basement windows that were covered. I listened but didn't hear anything. I moved further toward the back of the house. The pull-up door on the detached garage had a row of windows. I was leery of finding another scene like out at Stanley's. Just a garage: stacked boxes in one corner, lawnmower and tools in another. By the back porch was one of those oversized trash containers on wheels.

Technically, trash is okay to go through without a warrant once it's out at the curb for pick-up—which this wasn't. But I'm not a cop and didn't have a warrant anyway. I lifted the lid. On top was a filled kitchen-sized trash bag. Down the inside edge of the container was what looked like a video box. I reached in and pulled it out. It was the cover to "The Spy Who Loved Me" starring Roger Moore as James Bond. I pulled out the top bag of trash. Below that was the cover box to "Westward Ho." John Wayne sings? And below that were a dozen or so badly mangled, burned and charred videocassettes.

I replaced the trash, closed the lid and went onto the back porch. I didn't see anyone through the kitchen door window curtain and vaguely saw that the door to the basement was open. I opened the screen and slowly turned the kitchen doorknob. It wasn't locked. Then I heard footsteps and saw

Jeannie coming up out of the basement. I turned quickly away and leaned against the wall. I hoped she hadn't seen me.

I heard the basement door close and then something placed in the sink. The water turned on for a moment and then off. I heard Jeannie leave the room. I dared a look and didn't see her. I opened the door, eased into the kitchen and quickly moved to the basement door and down the stairs. It was dark. The windows were tightly covered, and the bit of light that seeped beneath the kitchen door didn't help much. I used a pencil flashlight to see. The air was stuffy, and as I descended the stairs I caught a whiff of stale urine. On a mattress and chained to pipes lay a man I hoped was Kenneth Stanley. He was on his side facing the wall and covered with a blanket. Nearby were two wooden chairs and a stool. On the stool lay a Bible opened to "The Revelation."

He stirred when I touched him.

"Not again," he murmured. "No more, please."

"I'm not Jeannie," I whispered. "I'm not Cameron."

He turned his face toward me. He hadn't shaved in more than a week, his eyes looked hollowed, but there was no doubt it was Kenneth Wayne Stanley. I shined the light on my face.

"I'm here to help you."

"Who . . . who are you?"

"Doesn't matter. Just know that you're going to be okay now."

The chain was tightly locked to Stanley's ankle with a padlock and secured with another to the main sewer pipe. The house was old, the pipe cast iron instead of modern PVC. There was no way I was going to break through that.

"Any chance the key to the padlock is down here?"

Stanley shook his head. "I don't know. Can you get me out of here?"

"Yes. You're getting out of here."

When? was the big question. I searched a nearby workbench for keys or a bolt cutter. All I found was a hacksaw. Better than nothing. Then it occurred to me that I had played this scene before. I didn't like the previous results. One didn't have to repeat one's mistakes. I didn't need to be the Lone Ranger. I called Carson.

The guy who answered said, "Did you say 'Carson'? Detective Carson's busy with an interview. Could you speak a little louder?"

"Sorry, I can't. How about Detective Jablowski or Captain Rodecker?"

"Jablowski's in the interview too, and the Captain's out. What's the problem? Can I help you?"

"Tell Carson this is Rachel Cord. I've found Kenneth Stanley. We're trapped in the MacPhersons' basement."

"Hold on."

"Rachel, this is Mike. Where are you?"

"In MacPherson's basement. I don't want to speak too loud, Jeannie's upstairs somewhere. Stanley's here. He's alive but chained to the wall. I don't know where Cameron is."

"We're interviewing Cameron now. Why are you there? You're supposed to be here with that tape, damn it."

"Chew me out later. I deserve it. Just get over here."

There were questions Stanley and I both wanted to ask, but it was too risky. So we waited quietly watching the strip of light beneath the door at the top of the stairs. I kept my gun ready in case Jeannie came down before the cavalry arrived. Every so often, I'd pat Stanley's arm to reassure him — and me — that everything would be all right. Thirty minutes later the doorbell rang, and Jeannie's footsteps crossed the floor above. There were murmured voices that were hard to make out. "You can't . . ." ". . . we can." More footsteps. Then the basement door opened, the light came on.

"Rachel? You down there?"

"Yes."

Mike Carson came down the stairs followed by a uniformed officer.

"We're over here. Stanley's chained. We need a key or

bolt cutters."

The officer went back up the stairs; Carson came over. From the look he gave me, I didn't want to hear his thoughts. He spoke to Stanley.

"Kenneth Stanley?"

"Yes."

"Are you hurt?"

"Don't think so. They didn't beat me or anything. I just feel so worn out. What day is it?"

"Tuesday, September seventh. Do you remember what happened? How you got here?"

"Not really. I remember having breakfast—at IHOP. Jeannie served me. I was woozy getting up. That was . . . you say it's the seventh? That's . . . Oh, God. Jerry. He's—"

"Jerry's fine." I touched Stanley's arm. "I found him. He's who sent us looking for you."

"Mr. Stanley," Carson said. "You were telling us what happened to you."

"Right. IHOP. I remember bumping a waiter. He dropped the food he was carrying. I think I apologized, but I'm not sure. I was having trouble focusing. Jeannie helped me to my car. I remember sitting down, but not in my car. My car was a few feet away. Someone was speaking, but . . . I can't remember what they said. Next thing I know I'm here and chained."

"They didn't hurt you? Threaten you?"

"Said I was going to Hell, mostly. Said they wanted to save me. Kept praying and reading the Bible. Trying to get me to repent. They burned all my videotapes. Things like that. Hard to remember, it's all jumbled together."

The officer came back, followed by two EMTs with a stretcher.

"That's enough for now," Carson said. "Let's get you out of here."

"Where's Cameron?" I asked.

"In holding. He broke down and confessed as soon as I

told him what you said on the phone."

As they put Stanley in an ambulance, I saw Jeannie sitting in the back of a police car. Jabba was leaning against the car writing in a pad. He looked over. I expected a caustic comment but he just shook his head. Mike walked me to my car and I gave him the tape.

"The missing tapes are in the trash can next to the back porch. They were destroyed."

"You should have told us what you thought. Let us handle it. This could have turned out different."

He didn't add "like last time," but I knew he thought it.

"You need to give us a statement. Can I trust you to follow us back to the station?"

That hurt. "Yes."

After giving my statement, getting another chewing out from Rod and being—not too politely—ordered to stay on my side of the river, I had almost enough time to make it to lunch with Wendy. As I went toward the bridge, I called Danny.

"We found your brother. He's okay."

"I know, thanks. Detective Jablowski just called. I'm headed to the hospital. Want to meet me there? I'd like to thank you *properly*, later."

I felt a blush coming. "Sounds tempting, but no thanks. I have other plans."

"Too bad. Whenever you change your mind, I'll be available, Rough Rider."

I hit the brake to keep from plowing into the car ahead of me. It took a few moments to compose myself and pay attention to what I was supposed to be doing—driving. Traffic moved along nicely. I called Carter to give him the good news as I crossed the river. I told him where Stanley was and said I'd have a final report to him in a day or two. Traffic was light on River Drive. It looked like I'd be only a few minutes late for lunch. I called Wendy.

"Hi. I know I'm late. Are you at Phil's yet?"

"Yes. I just ordered tea. Is this a habit I should get used

to?"

"No. I hate being late. I should be there in just a few minutes. We found Kenneth Stanley this morning. He's alive and been taken to the hospital. His kidnappers are in custody."

"Where was he?"

"I'll tell you about it when I get there."

"Okay. Oh, your ghost just arrived."

"What ghost?"

"Don't you remember? On our first date? That busboy you were staring at when you sat down. The one who reminded you of Karen. I'm looking at him right now. He's cleaning some tables across the room. You're right. He does look like Karen; or like those other women who were murdered. He could be their twin."

"The busboy?"

"Yes, the busboy. Give him a wig, women's clothes, a little make-up, who would know the difference?"

I remembered. I was starting to sit when I thought I saw Karen's face in the shadows. It was a busboy with a buzz cut. I had totally forgotten about him. The perfect disguise. Everyone's been looking for a woman. That was why he was standing outside of the restrooms at River Park: he was waiting for Mr. Jensen to look away so he could duck into the Men's room and get rid of his wig. It's why George, Margo and I didn't see a woman on the security cameras. Only a man with a buzz cut. It's why Helen couldn't find someone looking like Karen flying out of Jacksonville. Right. With a wig and clothing, who would know the difference? I lost track of what Wendy was saying.

"He sees me watching him. He's coming this way. See you when you get here."

"Wendy, don't hang up! Wendy! Stay away from him! WENDY!"

Twenty-Five

SHE HAD HUNG UP. I stomped on the accelerator. The speedometer eased up past its max of 85. I turned on the headlights and hazards and honked the horn as I wove in and out of traffic. I pressed, "Last call sent," and then "Send." After six rings, I got voicemail. I ended the call and speed-dialed Frank.

"Taylor here."

"Frank, the killer is the busboy at Phil's. He's there now. Wendy's in trouble."

"What are you talking about?"

"The one who killed Karen and Aiko and Evelyn and who knows how many others. We've been looking for a woman, but he's not a woman. He's a man. He dresses to look like his victims."

I was rattling off the top of my head as I cut in and out of traffic. I had to get there in time. I couldn't lose Wendy. That bastard couldn't steal from me again. Frank was talking.

". . . check it out. Where are you?"

"No time. Wendy's at Phil's. She saw him and reminded me of him on the phone. I think she's with him now, she said he was there before she hung up. She's not answering. He's going to kill her."

Frank said something to someone else and came back to me. "Where are you?"

"Almost there. I'm on River Drive approaching Cutter. I'll be at Phil's in a moment if I don't have an accident." HONK! HONK! "Get out of the way!"

"Rachel, units are on the way. Wait for us."

I couldn't wait. I couldn't lose someone else. I made the turn at Cutter and almost lost it. I could feel the back end sliding and the tire nudged the center median before I straightened out. A hubcap went spinning across the road. This was no time to be careless. I jammed the brakes and screeched to a stop in front of Phil's; reached in my bag on the seat beside me and removed my gun. I left the car in the street and ran into the Tearoom.

Elspeth was at the desk.

"Where's Wendy?" I yelled.

"In the back by the windows. What's wrong?"

I rushed through the room keeping my gun low and tight to my side so as not to scare anyone. I scanned the room. I didn't see Wendy. A tub of dirty dishes was on the table; so was Wendy's cell phone. I saw two waitresses but no busboy. I went straight for the alcove that led to the kitchen, back restrooms and a back exit.

I looked in the kitchen but didn't see Wendy or the busboy. I checked the restrooms. The women's room was empty. There was a man at the urinal in the men's room. No one else. I went down the hall. The door to the alley was closed and would set off an alarm if opened. A door to the left said "PRIVATE." I opened it. It was the back stairwell of the building. A woman's shoe lay on the second step. I rushed up the stairs.

The other shoe was on the second floor landing. The door was locked. Was it locked for them? Which way? Decide, damn it! I raced to the third floor. The door opened on an empty hallway. Office doors looked closed. Did they go this way? The only place above was Phil's apartment.

"Don't."

The muted voice came from above. I ran up the stairs. At the top of the stairs were an entry hall, elevator, front staircase and the open door to Phil's apartment.

I entered the foyer. Beyond to the left were the kitchen and dining room. To the right, a massive front room overlooked the street. Phil lay unmoving on the floor by a couch. I couldn't see if she were breathing or not. Tea things were scattered on the floor. Near the front window the busboy held Wendy as he looked out. Sirens in the distance were getting louder. Wendy twisted to get away from him.

"Let me go."

" She said, let her go."

He spun pulling Wendy in front of him. He held a knife against her body.

"Go away or I'll kill her."

It was hard to see much of him, part of his face, his arm. I kept my gun up in a two-handed grip, aiming as best I could as I moved closer.

"You're not killing anyone. Drop the knife. Let her go."

For a moment Karen's dark eyes stared at me. Pleading.

"This is your only chance to—"

"No! You go away. Now!"

He pulled Wendy's hair forcing her head back. He held the knife out, the tip pointing at her throat. Wendy's eyes were wide with fear. Could I risk a shot? Was I good enough to get him and not Wendy? Would he stab her if I failed? This man killed Karen. Might kill Wendy. I couldn't let that happen. I separated my hands, held the gun upward and backed a step.

"Take it easy. No one's dying here. Not now."

He relaxed his hold on Wendy's hair. She looked at me. I could see that she was going to do something. Wendy don't!

Wendy twisted and dropped to her left. The busboy stabbed at her. My gun fired. My round caught him in the shoulder, spun him back and around. He no longer had the knife. My second shot hit him full in the chest, sending him back into the window. I fired again. Glass shattered. I caught one glimpse of Karen's surprised expression on the busboy's face before he disappeared. Time stopped as I stared at the empty space, then rushed forward again.

I ran to Wendy lying on the floor, the knife protruding from her side.

Epilogue

IT FELT GOOD TO snuggle with someone again. It went a long way to easing the loss, the pain, the guilt. Wendy moved in her sleep and let out a soft grunt. Her wound was nearly healed but still pulled and pained whenever she moved the wrong way. She resettled in my arms, her head pillowed against my breast.

Karen was dead and gone. I wasted a year accusing her of running away, of trying to understand how I had wronged her to make her leave. The wronging was my accusations, the thinking that she had left.

We held a memorial service at Phil's for friends and family. Phil arranged everything. She was all right except for a lingering bruise on her temple where she'd been hit. Karen's paintings from our condo were displayed as well as several that Jacqueline Losey brought from Cramer College. Karen's ashes were there in a simple eighteenth century Japanese urn that her sister and brother, Tori and Robert, brought.

Tori and her husband, Michael Cisneros, and Robert and his wife Maiko sat in the front row with Wendy and me. Wendy should have stayed another day or two in the hospital but insisted on being there. I think she was afraid of the type of sympathy I may be offered. She may have been right.

Jackie's overtures to spend time with me were hardly subtle, but I would have resisted — even without knowing about her Wayne middle name. Danny was there too. Now, she would have been harder to resist.

Danny thanked me again for finding and helping her brother. Kenneth Stanley was mostly recovered from his ordeal, and he and Danny were reconciling. Danny might even move back into the family home, though she planned to continue to work at Puss 'n Boots; and Jerome Carter might move in too as his divorce progressed. I didn't want to guess how that threesome would work out.

I missed my appointment with Mavis Webb, but she understood given the circumstances. She said she could wait. She didn't have to wait long. Clarence was as predictable as I thought. It took only four days to get Mavis all the evidence she needed, and more than she wanted. It turned out that Clarence wasn't only having an affair with his secretary, but with Mavis's sister too.

Henry Seiko or Marvin Osaka or Shawn Endo, or whoever the busboy really was, still lay unclaimed at the county morgue. The police have yet to determine his true identity. In addition to his three male identities, the police discovered Social Security cards for 11 different women, including Karen, Aiko Nagasawa, Martinez and Ohara. Frank told me that law agencies in six states were involved in tracking the whereabouts of the missing women and men.

Wendy snuggled close. "Ouch." Another pinch in her side woke her.

"What time is it?"

"Three thirty."

Wendy sat up. Looked at me in the cool light reflecting in from the balcony. She gave me a leering grin and reached for my cell phone on the nightstand. Held it out to me.

I shook my head. "I don't need that anymore."

"But I want to know what I'm up against."

I shook my head again. Wendy checked the phone

directory and pressed "Send."

I heard Margo pick up on the third ring and immediately begin speaking in that deep rumble that vibrates my being. Wendy shook slightly then put the phone to my ear. I immediately shivered and softly moaned.

". . . *you hidden orchestras, you serenades of phantoms with instruments alert . . .*"

Wendy moved the phone away against the pillow, leaned in and whispered.

"I see what you mean." She tickled my ear with her tongue. "Maybe we'll keep Margo."

She put the phone back to my ear. Margo continued speaking.

"*You formless, free, religious dances . . .*"

His low vibes cut through me as Wendy kissed me, her lips slowly descending my body.

Acknowledgments

Writers may write in a vacuum, but they don't publish in one. My thanks and appreciation to first readers Amanda, J.C., Lee, Liz, Mel, and Bill Binkley. Their critical eye, suggestions and thoughts made this a better book. Any remaining errors are mine. A special thanks to Barbara Lane from Down Under for opening a franchise of Peaches Beauty Therapy in Rachel's city.

www.ingramcontent.com/pod-product-compliance
Lightning Source LLC
Chambersburg PA
CBHW071508170626
46811CB00007B/2765